JAMESON

HUNTER SQUAD
BOOK 1

ANNA HACKETT

Jameson

Published by Anna Hackett

Copyright 2025 by Anna Hackett

Cover by Hang Le Designs

Cover image by Wander Aguiar

Edits by Tanya Saari

ISBN (ebook): 978-1-923134-57-7

ISBN (paperback): 978-1-923134-58-4

This book is a work of fiction. All names, characters, places and incidents are either the product of the author's imagination or are used fictitiously. Any resemblance to actual persons, events or places is coincidental. No part of this book may be reproduced, scanned, or distributed in any printed or electronic form.

WHAT READERS ARE SAYING ABOUT ANNA'S ACTION ROMANCE

The Powerbroker - Romantic Book of the Year (Ruby) winner 2022

Heart of Eon - Romantic Book of the Year (Ruby) winner 2020

Cyborg - PRISM Award Winner 2019

Unfathomed and Unmapped - Romantic Book of the Year (Ruby) finalists 2018

Unexplored – Romantic Book of the Year (Ruby) Novella Winner 2017

Return to Dark Earth – One of Library Journal's Best E-Original Books for 2015 and two-time SFR Galaxy Awards winner

At Star's End – One of Library Journal's Best E-Original Romances for 2014

The Phoenix Adventures – SFR Galaxy Award Winner for Most Fun New Series and "Why Isn't This a Movie?" Series

Beneath a Trojan Moon – SFR Galaxy Award Winner and RWAus Ella Award Winner

Hell Squad – SFR Galaxy Award for best Post-Apocalypse for Readers who don't like Post-Apocalypse

"Like Indiana Jones meets Star Wars. A treasure hunt with a steamy romance." – SFF Dragon, review of *Among Galactic Ruins*

"Action, danger, aliens, romance – yup, it's another great book from Anna Hackett!" – Book Gannet Reviews, review of *Hell Squad: Marcus*

Sign up for my VIP mailing list and get your *free box set* containing three action-packed romances.

Visit here to get started: www.annahackett.com

CHAPTER ONE

HUNTER SQUAD

Jameson

"Get us in closer."

Holding the handgrip overhead, I looked out the open side door of the Talon quadcopter. Its four rotors droned quietly as we flew in over the dense Australian bush.

We were on the edge of the Blue Mountains, just inland of New Sydney.

And we were hunting a monster.

"Jameson, the creature is tracking northeast," a female voice said in my earpiece. It was our comms officer, Sasha.

"*There*." Beside me, Kaitoa Rahia pointed.

Kai was the same height as me, but leaner, and with black hair that he kept cut short. His Māori heritage was stamped all over his face. We often ran together, and the guy was fast. He also had quick instincts that had saved my ass too many times to count.

"I see it." I studied the flash of movement in the trees below. The thing was crashing through the vegetation. "Sasha, keep tracking it. We're going in."

The monster reached a clearing and I got a good view of it. It was like something out of a nightmare. It lumbered on four legs, its slow movements deceptive. It had a thick, scaly hide, and several razor-sharp spikes along its back.

I lifted my carbine and checked the charge on the laser weapon. "Hunter Squad, are you ready for some monster hunting?"

"Hell, yeah," my squad shouted back.

I met their gazes one by one. Like me, they all wore light-weight, gray combat armor. They were my squad mates, my friends, the people I trusted to always have my back. We'd grown up together in the ruins of a world destroyed by an alien invasion. Our parents had taught us grit, toughness, and determination.

Our parents had beaten the aliens. Now, we were helping to keep the rebuilding world safe from the horrors the aliens had left behind.

Zeke and Marc Jackson were twins, both six foot five and muscular. They looked identical, with brown skin and square jaws, but their personalities were the total opposite. Zeke was always scowling, while Marc was grinning, ear to ear.

North Connors was checking his small medical backpack. The ladies loved North, and frequently referred to him as tall, dark, and handsome. He was our squad medic, and had the steadiest hands and head out of all of us. He was dedicated, triple-checked everything, and rock solid in a crisis.

The final member was our latest recruit. Scott Simms had blond hair and pale skin, and was currently fidgeting with his carbine. He'd only been with us a few weeks, and I wasn't entirely sure he was going to make it. He was decent enough with a carbine, but he was nervous. I was keeping a close eye on him, and to be honest, I wasn't sure I trusted the kid to have my squad's back.

That was something my father had taught me—that you had to trust every member of your squad with your life. No hesitation. Marcus Steele had been the best squad leader ever. One day, I wanted to be as good as him.

"Colbie, swing us around," I ordered.

Our pilot glanced back from the cockpit. "On it, Jameson." There was a grin on her pretty face, her red hair peeking out from under her flight helmet. Then she turned the Talon on a dime, swinging the aircraft in over the clearing. No one could fly like Colbie Erickson. It was in her blood.

My gaze found the monster below, following its path through the trees. It had attacked a nearby town and injured three people. It had to be stopped.

"Hunter Squad—" I attached the rapid rappel line to my belt "—let's move out."

Kai and Scott flanked me, both checking their lines. I knew that behind me, on the other side of the Talon, Zeke, Marc, and North were doing the same.

"Go!" I leaped out of the quadcopter, Kai and Scott with me.

The rappel lines whizzed as we dropped toward the ground.

My boots hit the dirt, and with the push of a button, I disconnected the line. I whipped my carbine up and walked forward.

My squad formed around me.

"Let's do this," I murmured.

The monster turned and saw us. It threw its head back and roared.

I smiled and aimed my weapon.

We opened fire.

"Take that, asshole," Marc called out.

The monster shuddered under the impact, then turned and ran.

"Go," I roared, breaking into a sprint.

My squad raced through the trees. I pumped my arms, leaping over a fallen branch.

"We'll cut it off," Zeke yelled.

I nodded. "Do it."

He and his brother disappeared into the dense bush.

A moment later, I came out in another clearing. It was silent. No birds chirping, no rustling in the bushes.

The monster was here.

I met Kai's green gaze, and my best friend nodded. He was our best tracker. He dropped to one knee, studying the ground.

The creature couldn't hide forever.

Our parents had beaten the aliens by creating a weapon that had destroyed the reptilian Gizzida. But during their time on Earth, the aliens had liked to experiment. It was how they'd reproduced. In their labs, they'd spliced their DNA with the DNA of different animals... and humans.

Some of the hybrid creatures had survived the weapon's detonation. Now, they hid deep in the forests, lakes, and rivers. Breeding, mating, mutating further.

Every now and then, they crawled out of the shadows.

My squad and I were the ones that put them down.

I kept moving through the trees, scanning for any sign of the monster. I slapped a branch out of the way and spotted something else. A house. It was long-abandoned, with the roof caved in and the windows broken.

I lifted my hand and pointed.

Scott, Kai, and North followed me toward it.

"Looks pre-invasion." Scott's voice shook a little.

"Jameson, I see a heat signature to the west of your location," Sasha said, her voice clipped and focused. "Fifty meters." She was using satellite images to give us intel.

I swiveled to the west and saw a flash of movement. The monster crawled up the wall of the house to the roof.

"One o'clock," I barked.

The creature let out a roar and leaped.

Strange tentacles flared out from its neck.

I whipped my carbine up and fired. The others joined in. The creature screeched, flopping onto the ground. It rolled through the dirt, then leaped up and sprung...at Scott.

Hell.

The monster took the young soldier down, vomiting a sticky, gray substance all over him.

I ran, swinging my carbine onto my back, and leaped onto the monster. I was careful to avoid the spikes as I yanked out my combat knife.

Gripping the hilt, I slashed down with all my strength into the thick hide at the base of the monster's neck.

It spun, baring its fangs, and leaped off Scott's prone form. I held on tight, riding it like the wild brumby horse my friends had dared me to ride as a teenager. I'd damn-near broken my neck back then, but didn't plan to this time.

Come on. Gritting my teeth, I pushed the blade in harder.

"Jameson, get clear."

Zeke's shout had me leaping off the monster. I hit the ground and rolled.

My squad mate stepped into view, holding a boxy weapon with two probes on the front of it. Blue electricity crackled on the end.

He fired.

Electricity shot through the air and hit the creature, skating over its body. It jerked and shook. The rest of the squad fired their carbines.

I slid my knife back into its sheath. Another monster bites the dust.

Then, I caught movement out of the corner of my eye. Something had just darted into the abandoned house.

"There's another one," I called out. I jogged toward the door, sliding my carbine off my shoulder.

"Jameson, do not go into the house alone," Sasha's voice echoed in my ear. "Wait for backup."

I knew if she'd been here, and not hundreds of kilometers away at Squad Command, she'd be up in my face. One thing Sasha wasn't, was shy.

"I've got this, Sash."

My comms officer made an annoyed sound. "You knuckleheads never listen to me."

"Sure we do. Most of the time." I shoved open the door and it creaked.

Inside the house, everything was covered in a thick layer of dust. The place was abandoned, but there was furniture still in place, books on the shelves, shoes by the door. Someone, a family by the look of the toys tossed on the old rug, had called this home. I walked in carefully, my boot crunching on broken glass.

Where are you?

I hadn't gotten a good look at the monster, so I wasn't exactly sure what I was dealing with. I scanned around, then moved into the kitchen, then into another living area.

There was an old flat-screen TV on a low stand, a dusty couch, and a pair of armchairs with some of the stuffing pulled out. I guessed that some critter had gotten into it over the decades to make a home.

This family had probably run during the invasion. I wondered if they'd made it. My jaw tightened. Many hadn't. The Gizzida had killed billions of people.

But they hadn't wiped us out.

No, for all our flaws, humans had grit, and a strong instinct to survive.

Outside, I heard my squad shouting. No doubt they had the monster contained.

A floorboard creaked.

I whirled, lifting my weapon.

A huge, clawed hand knocked the gun out of my damn hands. It flew and hit the wall.

Fuck.

This monster was more humanoid than most. It had grayish-brown, scaly skin, and walked upright, on two muscular legs. I was six foot three, but it towered over me by a foot. Its muscles bulged, and it had overlong arms, and glowing red eyes.

It snarled and attacked.

It hit me like a fucking tank. I whipped an arm against its neck, holding off its snapping jaws. Its face was close to mine, and its breath smelled rank. It snarled, raw hunger glowing in its red eyes.

"Not today, asshole," I gritted out.

I whirled and rammed a punch into its midsection. Damn, it was like hitting a brick wall. Sasha was shouting in my ear, but I blocked her out.

Grinding my teeth together, I shoved. We spun, and the monster slammed me into the wall. Pain vibrated through my body.

Then it whirled and tossed me.

I crashed through a wooden coffee table, and hit the floor. Something twinged in my torso.

Swallowing a groan, I pushed up. A broken table leg was right in front of me. I snatched it up. The end of it was pointed and sharp.

The monster came at me with a roar.

I stabbed out with the table leg. It sunk into the thick flesh in the creature's midsection, and the beast roared.

"Yeah, you don't like that, do you?"

Its claws raked against my body armor. Then it pulled its fist back, and swung.

The blow sent me staggering back. My head slammed into the wall and my ears rang.

Shit.

I reached out, my fingers closing on the TV on the stand beside me. I gripped it hard, and with a huge swing, I aimed it at the monster.

The screen hit its head and shattered. The creature let out a garbled, angry sound.

I turned to run. A heavy blow hit my back, and I crashed to the floor facefirst.

Shit. The air rushed out of me, my ribs hurting. Then I lifted my head, and spotted my carbine on the floor, just ahead of me.

Yes. I stretched out an arm. My fingers brushed the end of it. The monster's steps made the floor vibrate.

Fuck. I stretched even more.

My fingers closed on the carbine, and I rolled onto my back.

The monster lunged at me, and I pressed the trigger. I fired right in its face.

Gore and blood splattered me.

Suddenly, more carbine fire joined mine.

Kai walked into the room, his expression deadly.

The monster landed heavily on my legs. Dammit, that hurt. I kicked the dead weight off me.

"Fuck," I muttered.

Kai walked over and held a gloved hand out.

I took it and let him haul me up.

"I hate when they're humanoid," Kai said.

"Me, too."

We both knew it meant that this creature had some human DNA. The Gizzida had held hundreds of thousands—maybe millions—of people in their labs. Done terrible things to them.

I blew out a breath. "Thanks."

Kai lifted his chin.

"Is he still alive?" Sasha's sharp voice.

I met Kai's gaze. His unique brilliant green eyes that he'd inherited from his mother were alight with amusement.

I shot him the finger. Yeah, we both knew that our comms officer would give me a mouthful about going in alone and ignoring her when we got back to base.

"I'm still breathing," I said.

Sasha's harsh expulsion of air came across the line. "You're supposed to *listen* to me, Jameson Steele."

"I do, Sasha. I promise I do."

She made a grumbling sound.

Kai and I headed for the front door. "Is the monster contained?"

"Yeah. It's dead."

"Scott okay?"

Kai winced. "Ah, no. Not sure he's gonna make it on the squad."

Damn. When we stepped outside, I spotted Scott sitting on the ground. He was fine, but his expression was vacant, and he was still covered in sticky, gray monster goo.

North was with him. We often teased North for being pretty, but the guy was a hell of a medic. He had a calm demeanor that people responded to. He was a trained doctor, and I was secretly glad he also liked being a soldier.

The twins were slicing bits off the monster. Zeke was named for their uncle who had died during the invasion. Marc was named after my father, Marcus.

"Quit that, you two," I called out.

Marc held up a fang and grinned. "These are worth good money."

I stomped forward, hiding my limp. My hip hurt like hell and my ribs were throbbing. Dammit, it probably meant a trip to the infirmary when we got home.

"Call Colbie," I said. "Let's get out of here. I need a beer."

Kai moved into step beside me. "You're hurt."

"I'll get it looked at when we get back. It's nothing to worry about."

"You need more than a beer. You need to get laid."

I scowled at him. "Says the man who never gets laid."

Kai shrugged a shoulder. "I'm choosy."

No, he wasn't. He'd had the same problem as me. We both wanted women who were off-limits.

My thoughts turned to blonde hair, light blue eyes with dark eyelashes, and a wide smile. My pulse jumped.

Then I squashed it.

I wasn't going there.

The woman I wanted was too smart for me, married

to her job, and a family friend. Hell, she was one of my best friends. We'd grown up together, and I had no right thinking of her the way I did.

I couldn't remember the exact moment that I suddenly realized that Greer Baird had breasts, but it was some time in our teenage years. We'd gone swimming at the river, our parents on duty to keep an eye out for monsters. Greer had shed her clothes to reveal a tiny, blue swimsuit…and looking at her had felt like being hit with a ton of bricks.

As we'd grown, I'd also come to appreciate her sharp mind, her focus, and her dedication to her engineering work.

She was a good friend. I called her parents uncle and aunt.

I shook my head. Greer didn't look at me that way, anyway. Not once. It was for the best. I'd forced myself not to call her lately. She had her boyfriend. I controlled a grimace. The asshole was nowhere good enough for her.

Some distance would help me get my head on straight where Greer was concerned.

The Talon came into view overhead.

"Let's go home, people. The beers are on me."

CHAPTER TWO

HUNTER SQUAD

Greer

"All right, get that equipment over there. We'll start reinforcing the next level."

As I issued the orders, my team moved to carry them out. I rested my hands on my hips, studying the dam wall that we were renovating and reinforcing.

I dragged in a deep breath and took in the view. The water gleamed, and a sea of native Australian trees flanked it on either side. The sun was hot overhead, but I knew that storms were forecast for later in the day.

I watched several workers wearing light exo-suits walking across the dam wall, carrying heavy blocks and equipment. The metal suits were worn like a second skeleton—running along the arms, legs and spine—and gave the users increased strength and agility.

The entire dam was a hive of activity. The first dam had been built here hundreds of years ago, but had been updated over the years. We were in charge of rebuilding and enhancing the dam wall, and adding in a hydroelectric power station. We were building on top of the old wall that had been damaged in the invasion. One side was the placid waters of the dam, and on the other, there were several spillway chutes that fed down into the Warragamba River.

Once, the Warragamba Dam had been the main water source for Sydney and the surrounding communities, as well as one of the world's largest domestic water supply dams.

It would be again. It was vital to rebuild our core infrastructure.

I was the chief engineer on this project. My first large, solo project. I watched a crane swinging overhead. They were setting more gear down.

This was the biggest job I'd ever been in charge of. I loved building, creating, and knowing I was doing my bit to help rebuild the world. Once the dam was operational again, it would be a secure water source for New Sydney. For years, the surrounding communities had been relying on rainwater and temporary filtration systems to gather water from the rivers. Growing up, I'd known that summertime meant we'd need to conserve water and sometimes ration it.

I glanced to the east. In the distance lay the ruins of the city of Sydney, once the largest city in Australia. During the invasion, bombs had rained down and an alien ship had landed there.

My parents had told me the stories of the invasion, and the fighting that had come afterward.

Most of the city had been destroyed and millions of

people had died. It was the same story across the world. Around the globe, the Gizzida had attacked and destroyed.

But humanity hadn't given up, even in the darkest moments. No, they'd fought back and won.

Rebuilding, however, was a slower process. Three decades on, and we were still working on it. The small towns were growing, transport routes were being built and upgraded, infrastructure put in place. We were rebuilding and upgrading the systems for power, agriculture, industry, and science.

"Greer?" One of my team called out. "Where do you want these stabilizers?"

"Over there, Sam." I pointed. "I want them ready for installation tomorrow."

The young man nodded, then turned to bark out orders to the others.

I walked along the edge of the wall. On my left, the dark, still waters, and on my right, the dizzying drop of concrete down to the river below.

Excitement trickled through me. This was an important project and I was going to make it a success. Breathing deeply, I turned back to the dam. The water was nestled in the bushland and while only a few hundred meters across, I knew that farther upstream it was wider, forming Lake Burragorang.

Suddenly, the middle of the pool rippled, and my heart rate spiked. My mouth flattened as I watched something—something big—move through the water.

It definitely wasn't a fish.

The humans had won the war. They'd beaten the aliens and killed them with a high-tech weapon.

But the Gizzida had managed to leave some things behind.

Creatures with some alien DNA melded with the local wildlife had survived the weapon. The monsters lived hidden in the shadows. Mutating and breeding.

I'd seen that ripple for a few days now. Disquiet made my chest tighten. I hadn't seen what it was, but I got the sense that it was watching us.

I dragged in a deep breath. The monsters were why we had the security squads. The most famous of all—Hunter Squad. I had lots of friends on the squad.

My thoughts turned to the squad leader—Jameson. Big, muscled, solid Jameson. He was the most sensible and trustworthy guy I knew. We'd grown up together and he was one of my good friends.

He had the best smile. And anytime I saw him with a shirt off…

I felt a pulse of heat.

"Stop it, Greer," I muttered. "You're *friends*. He's practically like a brother."

Except I didn't think of Jameson Steele in any brotherly way.

I straightened. He wasn't interested in me in that way. He'd never shown the slightest hint he saw me as anything other than a friend.

Besides, I was focused on my work. My important work.

My nose wrinkled. My last relationship hadn't ended well. Toby was another engineer. He was smart, good at his job, and we'd dated for about six months. The sex had been good, and the conversation riveting. We had our work in common. We could talk complex engineering for hours.

Then he'd told me about how I needed to give up my work and have lots of his babies. That it was our duty to help repopulate the world and pass on his superior genes.

Ugh.

Jameson's image popped back into my head. He was rugged, and a little rough around the edges. Sex wouldn't be good with Jameson, it would be something else entirely.

I frowned. I hadn't heard from him in over a month. Usually, we called every week and caught up when I was home for a beer or dinner at one of our parents' houses.

Lately, I felt like Jameson was avoiding me. Maybe because the last time I'd seen him, Toby had been with me. The three of us had gone out for dinner and Toby had been an obnoxious twat. He'd made it clear that he thought any work that didn't require an advanced degree not worthy of his time or discussion. He'd even called Jameson a grunt.

Jameson had stayed silent as Toby had prattled on. Honestly, it had been the death knell for our relationship. I'd broken up with Toby ten days later.

My communicator vibrated on my belt, cutting through my thoughts. I pulled it out, then stretched the screen into a larger size. We still didn't have a full cellular phone system like before the invasion, but key locations in the area had comms beacons that linked to our growing satellite system.

I touched the screen and my father's face came into view. I smiled. "Hi, Dad. Handsome as ever."

"Hi, baby girl."

I had to admit Shaw Baird was good-looking, even if he was my dad. His blond, shaggy hair had some gorgeous silver in it. He was tanned and his grin held a touch of mischief.

"How's my favorite daughter?" he asked.

"I'm your only daughter."

"Fine. You're my favorite child."

I snorted. "I know you tell Ethan he's your favorite when you call him." My brother was a tech specialist who could make any computer sing.

My dad just smiled. "How's your dam project coming along?"

"Good. Still a lot of work to do." I glanced at the water. It was now as smooth as glass. "Hopefully we'll have no delays."

Dad's brows drew together. "What's bothering you?"

"Nothing."

"Greer, I can read you like an open book. I know when something's worrying you."

"It's probably nothing. I've seen something moving in the water. Something big."

Dad's face snapped into serious in the blink of an eye. "Call Jameson."

"Dad, I didn't get a good look at it. I don't want to overreact."

"Just call him, and give him a heads-up. He's the expert when it comes to monsters."

Or at least the expert when it came to killing them. "All right."

"Good. Any chance you can get home soon for dinner? Your mother misses you."

My mom was busy training new recruits at the New Sydney Military Academy. My parents were both former soldiers, part of the infamous Hell Squad, who'd been instrumental in defeating the aliens.

To the rest of the world, they were both legends, but to me, they were Mom and Dad. Mom was a badass soldier, and dad was a brilliant sniper. He trained recruits at the Academy, as well.

"Maybe I can make it for a quick visit. If I can make it happen, I'll let you know."

"Good." He glanced to the side. "I've got to go. Marcus is here. We're going to drive into New Sydney to check security at some power installations."

Marcus was Jameson's father. "Say hi to Uncle Marcus."

"Will do. He'd like to see you too, baby girl. Come home soon."

"Love you, Dad."

"Love you back."

I lowered the communicator just as someone called out my name. *Time to get back to work.*

As I turned, I glanced at the water one last time.

It was smooth and still.

Yep, I was clearly overreacting.

Still, this would give me the perfect excuse to talk to Jameson.

Jameson

FEELING MORE human after my shower, I pulled on fresh cargo pants and a T-shirt. I noticed a hole in the bottom of my shirt.

Damn. It was one of my favorites. I wasn't ready to recycle it, yet. We'd all grown up more frugal and careful than the stories I'd heard of life before the invasion. Fast fashion wasn't a thing anymore.

I'd been held up in the infirmary way longer than I'd hoped. But all my injuries were healed up, thanks to a shot of nano-meds. I poked my ribs and didn't feel a twinge. The microscopic machines could heal up just about anything.

I headed out of my house.

My teammates and I all had wooden eco-houses on the edge of the town of Dawn. It was built above an underground base called the Enclave, inland of the coastal town of Wollongong. We were about an hour south of New Sydney.

After the invasion, some people had moved back to the ruins of Sydney, and started growing the new town. Others—like my parents—had stayed here and built Dawn. It was nestled amongst beautiful hills and rolling green fields, surrounded by a large security wall that kept out the monsters. It had been a good place to grow up.

The Squad Command headquarters were close by. All the squads were based there. Most were tasked with general security, acting as law enforcement and providing security for the entire area.

Some of the older invasion survivors still lived underground in the Enclave. A number of them were too afraid to live above ground, even though the aliens were long gone, and the walls held the monsters at bay.

I walked to the house beside mine, and knocked on Kai's door. Like me, my best friend was the son of a soldier. Tane Rahia had led Squad Three, better known as the berserkers. The tales about their exploits were wild. Tane was still scary and intense, and my father claimed Tane was one of the best soldiers he'd ever fought beside.

Smiling, I shook my head. The berserkers were all still hellraisers, especially when they got into a bottle of bourbon. Uncle Hemi, Kai's uncle, owned a local distillery, and the bar in Dawn.

Kai appeared, looking very much like his dad.

"We're meeting the others at Hemi's," I told him.

Kai lifted his chin. "I need a beer."

"Me, too."

He pulled his door shut and the electronic lock beeped. We walked down the street. It was lined with more modular houses like ours—small, compact, and environmentally friendly. The engineers had designed them to be strong, and easy to build.

I glanced up. Dawn was surrounded by a fifteen-foot wall with watchtowers and guards evenly spaced along it.

Early on, monster attacks had been common. But over the years, the squads had thinned them out. Now, the remaining monsters tended to keep to the more remote parts of the bush, but the town couldn't afford to let its guard down. No one wanted kids getting pulled off bikes, or farmworkers getting eaten.

My job was to be a shield between the monsters and people. I was good at it. All I'd ever wanted was to be like my dad. I'd hated school, and sitting in a classroom, and reading books. I'd always preferred to be outside, using my hands, doing something,

We turned a corner and Hemi's bar came into view. Several tables sat outside of the building. Music was pumping from the inside.

Zeke and Marc sat at one of the tables out front. They already had beers in front of them.

As we approached, two women crossed the street to intercept us.

"Jameson!" My mom smiled up at me.

"Hey, Mom." Elle Steele was still beautiful. She'd raised three rambunctious kids, and was the most giving person I'd ever met. She'd been the comms officer for Hell Squad, which was how my parents had met. She was tougher than her slim form suggested.

I hugged her.

"I heard you had a call out," she said. "And you went into a situation alone, without back up."

I glanced at the woman with my mom.

Sasha grinned back. It was her father's wide smile. Sasha Rahia was short, curvy, and sassy as hell. She had a wild mane of black, curly hair, and smooth, brown skin. "I may have given her an update. Comms officer to former comms officer."

"I had everything under control," I assured my mom.

"You got hurt." Worry filled her eyes.

"It was just a few bruises. I've been to the infirmary. One-hundred-percent healthy."

I wasn't going to mention the cracked ribs and swelling on my hip that the nano-meds had healed up. I knew she'd just worry.

My mom sighed. "Just like your father, always downplaying things." She frowned. "You have a hole in your shirt." She poked at it. "Bring it to me later and I'll mend it for you."

"Thanks, Mom. Where are you headed now?"

My mother smiled. "I'm doing story time at the Enclave creche."

I knew she loved to volunteer with the little kids at the day care. "I'll walk you over."

Smiling, she slid her arm through mine. "Bye, Sasha."

"Bye, Aunt Elle." Sasha looked at me. "I'll have a cold beer waiting for when you get back."

I gave her a chin lift. Mom and I walked down the street. Colorful flowers filled some of the garden beds. My guess was they were the doing of Kai's sister. The woman loved flowers and had a green thumb. She worked on the agricultural team, growing crops.

"You're sure you're all right?" Mom asked.

"I'm fine, Mom. I promise."

She patted my arm. "It's my job to worry about you. I did it when you were a baby, and when you were a fearless toddler who climbed everything, and now, even though I know you're an adult, I'm not going to stop."

I dropped a kiss to the top of her head.

We reached the entrance to the Enclave base. We

passed some people coming out, who nodded and said hello, then we headed down the stairs.

The Enclave didn't feel like an underground base. Built in an old coal mine, it had touches of luxury, including priceless art on the walls that had been saved during the invasion. There was a swimming pool that was popular with the kids and a state-of-the-art lighting system that mimicked natural light. Large skylights had been fitted as well, which Mom had told me hadn't been there in the early days. Most of it was offices for people from all jobs—power generation, medical, teaching, law enforcement, government.

We followed the corridor to the creche. Workers left their kids here when they were on shift. Through the glass wall, I saw a bunch of them of various sizes in lots of different colors. They were running around, squealing and laughing.

Mom pushed the door open, and waved at some of the staff. Then the kids spotted her.

"Ms. Elle!" a little girl cried.

A group of them ran at Mom, throwing their arms around her jean-clad legs.

"Hello, my munchkins." She ruffled hair and smiled. Then I saw her sign hello to a little boy. I spotted a small cochlear implant on the side of his head. "Who's ready for story time?"

I leaned against the doorframe and watched as she settled into a chair. She was so good with them. She had this calming aura that I'd loved as a kid. But she still had a spine of steel. She stood up to my dad and could dig in when she wanted to.

The kids all dropped to sit on a large, colorful rug. Some of them were solely focused on Mom, while others fidgeted and twitched. That had been me as a kid. Sitting still had not been a skill of mine.

"Ms. Elle, can you tell the story about the invasion?" a girl asked.

"Yes, the Gizzida invasion." A little boy curled his hands like claws and let out a small roar.

Mom smiled. "I've told that story so many times."

The little girl pouted. "We want it again."

Another girl clasped her hands together. "Pleeeeease."

"All right. Many years ago, a huge alien ship appeared in the sky. Bombs fell and the Gizzida tried to take our planet."

"They looked like dinosaurs," a boy added.

"That's right. They were reptilian, and led by the raptors." Mom's voice deepened. "But, humans weren't going to give up." She looked at the kids one by one. "We wanted to protect our family and friends, we wanted to fight for our home. We wanted to survive."

"Hell Squad protected people," a boy piped up. "They fought the aliens."

"Yes," a girl said. "Marcus, Cruz, Gabe, Reed, Shaw, and Claudia." She recited the names, ticking them off on her fingers.

"That's right," Mom said. "Hell Squad was tough. They were brave and selfless and never backed down from a fight."

"And Squad Nine helped too," a girl said. "They had lots of lady soldiers."

A boy bounced up and down. "And the Berserkers. My dad said they were rough and wild."

I fought a smile and saw Mom doing the same. "Your dad is right, but those wild berserkers also were tough and courageous. But it wasn't just the squads who helped us survive. It was the pilots, the mechanics who fixed things, the technicians, and the engineers who kept us with power and water. It was the doctors and nurses and teachers. The brave people who scavenged for food and supplies, and the people who cooked the food. Everyone was brave, even when they were afraid, and did their part. Eventually, a weapon was designed. One that defeated the Gizzida. Then, we were safe."

The kids cheered.

"But the monsters stayed behind." A little girl shivered.

"I'm scared of the monsters," another girl whispered.

Mom reached for her and settled the girl on her lap. "You don't need to be afraid. Yes, the monsters the Gizzida created stayed, but Dawn has a big wall around it and guards, as do all the other towns. But best of all we have—"

A boy shot to his feet. "Hunter Squad!"

Mom flicked me an amused glance. "That's right. We have the very brave and well-trained soldiers on the security squads, especially Hunter Squad, who track down the monsters. They protect us and keep us safe." She leaned forward. "Did you know the leader of Hunter Squad is my baby?"

The girl on her lap scrunched her face up. "A baby can't be a soldier."

"No, my baby is all grown up. Boys and girls, I'd like you to meet my son, Jameson, the leader of Hunter Squad."

The kids' heads all whipped around and I saw a sea of faces peering at me, all with their mouths open.

"You're the boss of Hunter Squad?" a boy asked in awe.

I straightened. "I am. And I promise you, my squad and I do everything we can to keep the monsters away."

"Do you have a carbine?" a girl asked.

I saw the warning look in Mom's eyes. Right, no gory details. "Yes. We have lots of weapons we use."

"Do you explode the monsters?" a boy asked, his face animated.

I cleared my throat. "The important thing is that Hunter Squad will always keep you safe."

"Can you all say thanks to Mr. Jameson?" my mom said.

"Thanks, Mr. Jameson," they all said in sing-song voices.

"Now, how about we draw some pictures?" Mom suggested.

"I'm gonna draw a big monster with huge claws." A boy raced to the small tables at the back of the room.

Mom smiled and walked over to me. "Thanks, Jameson. I like to keep them informed without scaring them." She hugged me again. "Dinner tomorrow night. Your father's grilling."

I winced. "He burns everything."

She smiled, love on her face. "I know. So be there to

make sure he doesn't. Your brother and sister will be there, too."

I hadn't seen my siblings for a couple of weeks. "If I don't get called out, I'll be there."

"Good. Love you."

I leaned down so she could kiss my cheek. As she hurried off to rejoin the kids, I spun and headed down the corridor.

The kids seemed a lot more carefree than we'd been as kids. We'd done security drills, just in case monsters breached the walls or the Gizzida returned. In my early years, Dad had always been alert, on guard. I still had memories of him wandering the house at night, checking that everything was okay. I guess after years of fighting for your survival, it took a long time for your battle readiness to fade.

Soon, I neared Hemi's. I could hear Marc's laughter half a block away.

"There he is," Sasha said.

I turned a chair around and sat down, leaning my arms across the top of it.

"Here, J." Zeke pushed a glass of beer into my hand.

"Thanks."

There were quite a few people in Hemi's, a good number of them agricultural workers. I took a long sip of the beer and savored it. Hemi had a good brewing team and they were always experimenting. They'd found a way to make the alcohol metabolize quickly and not leave any aftereffects.

"Where's Colbie?" I asked.

Marc snorted. "That woman won't leave her damn

Talon alone. Said she wanted to get some systems checks done. She'll stop by if she isn't too late."

A woman walked into the bar, and Zeke stiffened, his gaze locking on her.

"Your sister's here," I said to Kai.

Amaia Rahia looked nothing like her brother. She was tall and slim, with pale skin, and a shock of white-blonde hair. She took after their mother, Selena—who happened to be an alien. Thankfully not of the reptilian kind.

"Hello, brother," Amaia said.

Kai lifted his hand. "Hey, sis."

She smiled at the rest of us. "Hunter Squad."

"Hey, Amaia," I said.

Her gaze flicked to Zeke. "Hi, Zeke."

He gave her a chin lift.

"How are things?" I asked.

"Going well." A smile broke out on her face. "Our latest crop is exceeding growth expectations."

That was Amaia, always happy, especially if her beloved plants were doing well.

"That's great."

Her ag team called out to her from a table inside. "I've got to go." She touched Kai's shoulder, and shot Zeke one last glance.

"Where's Scott?" I asked.

At the end of the table, North sighed. "He quit."

Ah, hell. "Is he okay?"

North nodded. "Physically, he's fine. Mentally, not so much. I don't think monster hunting is for him."

I rubbed the back of my neck. "I'll check in on him, then start looking at new recruits."

My comm dinged, and I pulled it off my belt. My heart leaped. It was a message from Greer.

Hey, Jameson. Can I call you later? It's work-related, and I need your advice.

I tapped in a reply.

Sure.

Well, I really knew how to keep the conversation going.

Thanks so much.

A server set more drinks down. The curvy brunette handed me a glass and a coaster. As she did, she held my gaze.

When I glanced down, I saw her comm number on the coaster. I gave her a small smile and sipped my drink. As she walked away, I let my gaze take her in.

She was gorgeous, but unfortunately, I didn't feel a blip of attraction.

Instead, I was thinking about when Greer would call. *Greer Baird is* not *for you.*

I quickly lifted my beer and drank it.

CHAPTER THREE

HUNTER SQUAD

Greer

"Get those supplies roped down." The wind whipped at my face, tearing at my hair and clothes.

The storm had come in fast. The wind was so strong that I was struggling to stay on my feet. My team and I were trying to secure all the construction supplies.

Everyone hurried around the dam wall, tying gear down and carrying crates into storage. The crane had been secured, and I hoped it didn't rip free. I glanced over at it, and watched it rocking in the wind.

Lightning flared through the sky, followed by a deafening crack of thunder. Even though I knew it was afternoon, it looked like night had fallen. The water looked dark and menacing, the tips of it flicked up into a frenzy. Overhead, the clouds boiled.

I pulled a mesh net over some boxes and clicked it down.

A cry pierced the deafening roar of the wind. Whipping around, I watched boxes tumbling down off the wall and into the water.

Dammit.

Pushing against the wind, I headed in that direction. There was another flash of lightning followed by a crack of thunder. I saw one of my engineers—I could tell it was Travis by his tall, lanky body and the hat he always wore—fighting against the wind.

Then the rain started.

It pelted down and I was drenched in an instant. Great, just great. I swiped water out of my eyes. Visibility turned to crap. I held my arm up, shielding my face.

I pushed on, and almost collided with one of my other engineers, Sam. He was fighting to get a rope tied over some crates. I rushed to help him, blocking one crate from sliding away with my hip.

"The storm wasn't forecast to be this bad," Sam yelled. His blonde hair was stuck to his head.

"Secure the gear, then we need to get everyone inside."

Suddenly, the rope flew out of his hand, flopping around. Together, we grabbed at it.

"Where's Travis?" I yelled. "I just saw him here."

"I don't know. He was going to get more rope."

Together, Sam and I got the rope tied down.

I straightened and scanned the wall. "Travis? Travis?"

There was no answer, only more thunder. I doubted he'd be able to hear me, even if he was right beside me. A crack of lightning illuminated the top of the wall. I didn't see anybody.

Where was he?

"Greer! Look!"

At Sam's shout, I spun. A coiled rope lay on the ground at the edge of the dam wall. Beside it, were Travis' hat and communicator. The man loved his stupid, beaten-up straw hat.

What the hell? I scanned the water.

"Do you think he fell?" Sam's voice was filled with worry.

My heart pounded in my chest. I hoped not. "Travis!"

Suddenly, something long and dark flew out of the water.

I staggered back and tripped, landing on my butt. Beside me, Sam cursed.

A huge, black tentacle slapped onto the dam wall beside me. It was oil-slick black and covered in bumps.

God. My pulse spiked, my heart hammering fast. I crawled backward. "Sam, get inside!"

"What about Travis?"

Something told me that Travis hadn't made it. I locked down the churning emotions inside me. I had to get Sam to safety.

"Go!" I shouted.

Sam ran, pumping his arms. The door to the interior base was at the end of the dam wall. Inside the wall was the power station, dam equipment, and living areas for the dam workers.

More lightning flared overhead. The water churned angrily, and a second tentacle arrowed into the dark sky.

Jesus, how big was the damn monster?

The tentacle beside me withdrew, slithering back into the water. I pushed to my feet. The roiling water seemed to expand, moving down along the dam wall.

Oh, no. It was following Sam.

"Sam, stop! Stay still."

The wind snatched my words away. He couldn't hear me.

No.

I looked around and spotted a toolbox. I quickly fumbled to open it, wiping away the water in my eyes. I grabbed a wrench and a hammer.

Turning, I sprinted down the dam wall. I leaped onto some crates and jumped off.

"Sam!"

A tentacle speared up. In horror, I watched it snap out and hit Sam.

The young engineer fell, hitting the concrete hard. It was clear he was winded. He looked back over his shoulder and his gaze met mine.

Then, the tentacle wrapped around his leg. It dragged him toward the water.

"*No.*" I ran toward him. I brought a hammer down and hit the tentacle hard.

It jerked side to side, slamming Sam into a box.

"Let him go." I threw the wrench toward the water.

The tentacle retracted fast. Sam screamed.

It lifted him into the air, then the man and tentacle dropped, and disappeared into the water.

My heart thudded in my ears and my lungs constricted like they were being squeezed by giant hands.

No. Sam. *God, no.*

"Greer?" I heard shouts and the thud of running footsteps. Two of my team appeared—Lisa and Kiaan.

"Everyone inside." I swallowed. "No one is to come out on the wall." My stomach clenched hard. "A monster in the water took Travis and Sam. We need help."

"Oh, God," Lisa cried, pressing a hand to her mouth. Her brown braid whipped around her slim shoulders.

Kiaan's face crumpled. He was several years older than me and our hydroelectric expert.

I ushered them both toward the door. As we stepped inside the dam base, Lisa grabbed my arm.

"Wait, Frankie and Jordan were locking down the exo-suits."

My chest squeezed. "They're still out there?"

Lisa nodded.

"Okay." I blew out a breath. Frankie was a good friend. I tried not to let my fear overwhelm me. "You two stay in here and keep the rest of the workers calm. I'll get them." I quickly pulled out my communicator. I needed to make a call before I went to find Frankie and Jordan. I stabbed at the screen.

"Hey, Greer," a deep voice said. "I thought you were calling later."

The familiar rumble of Jameson's voice felt like a calm in the storm. I turned on the video.

His rugged face appeared on the screen, then he frowned. "You okay? You're all wet."

"No, I'm not okay. Jameson...I need Hunter Squad. I need you."

Jameson

THE WIND BUFFETED THE TALON.

I gripped the handhold above my head to keep my balance.

"This storm is bad," Zeke muttered.

The others were sitting, but I couldn't. I was standing, fighting to keep my balance and staring out at the rain-drenched darkness that we were flying over.

Greer was in trouble.

My fingers flexed on the handhold. I had to get to her.

"What did Greer say about this monster?" Kai asked.

"Not much. It was in the water and it had tentacles." I gritted my teeth. "It took two of her people."

"Hell," North said.

I prayed that Greer was inside and safe.

"I have a visual," Colbie yelled from the cockpit. "But the visibility is crap in this rain."

A huge gust of wind hit us, and the Talon shuddered.

The squad was tense but ready. I hated that we were a soldier down. I needed to replace Scott, but we couldn't stop helping people when they needed it.

"Oh, God," Colbie said.

Not much rattled my pilot. I shoved forward and leaned into the cockpit. I barely paid any attention to

Colbie as she worked the controls. She could handle the bad weather.

She was the daughter of two pilots. Finn had been Hell Squad's Hawk pilot. Hawks were the quadcopter model that came before the Talons. Finn still trained new pilots, and Lia, Colbie's mother, was still in charge of the drone pilots, like she had been during the alien invasion. Now, the drones delivered goods to communities all around the area, rather than dropping bombs.

Colbie was the best pilot I knew. If anyone could handle this storm, it was her.

I looked ahead. The gray dam wall stood out in the darkness. Then I cursed.

Two giant tentacles were slapping at the wall.

And then I saw Greer.

My gut locked. "The little idiot."

She had a blaster in her hand and was shooting at the monster. Running my gaze quickly along the wall, I spotted two people huddled by some crates. The monster was between them and Greer.

"All right, Hunter Squad." I turned to my team, checking my armor. "We have three people on the dam wall, and one nasty, aquatic monster with tentacles."

My guys checked their carbines, getting ready.

Marc smiled. "Only one monster? Easy."

"Get us in there, Colbie," I ordered.

"On it, boss man."

I wrenched open the side door. The wind and rain flew at my face, but I ignored it. "Let's move."

As soon as the Talon was over the dam wall, I jumped.

I landed, bent my knees, and whipped my carbine up.

My team moved in beside me. We opened fire on the creature, our lasers lighting up the night. The monster let out an ear-splitting noise, its tentacles waving madly.

Shit. I needed to get Greer clear.

"Concentrate fire on the center of mass," I shouted.

Even if they couldn't hear me over the wind, my orders would come through their earpieces. My squad moved closer to the edge of the dam wall. I lowered my weapon and ran toward Greer.

"*Jameson*." Her hair was plastered to her head.

I hauled her close. "You need to get inside."

"Not without my people."

I turned my head to look at the two people trapped on the far side of the wall.

"Come on." I waved at the man and woman.

They rose and took one step.

A black tentacle slapped down between us.

I swiveled my carbine and fired. The tentacle jerked, but didn't move away. I saw the terror on the man and the woman's faces. They were frozen.

"Get inside, Greer. I'll get your people."

"No." She straightened and aimed her blaster. "I'll help."

"Greer—"

"You're wasting time, Jameson."

Dammit. I advanced on the tentacle, firing. Beside me, Greer fired her blaster.

The tentacle slid toward us. I tackled Greer and

rolled us out of the way. I ended up on top of her, the rain hammering down on us.

"Okay?"

She licked her lips and nodded.

Rising, I pulled her to her feet. Then I yanked my combat knife from the sheath on my thigh.

I was going to have to get up close and personal.

"Stay behind me." I strode over and rammed the blade into the tentacle. I yanked, opening up a gash.

The tentacle went mad. I used all my strength, cutting and hacking. Thick, black blood oozed from the wound. Damn, the skin was thick. Gritting my teeth, I kept pulling the knife through the tentacle.

Hands gripped mine and Greer was there, adding her strength to mine.

Together, we sawed the blade through the thick flesh. The tentacle ripped free, leaving a hunk of it behind. It flopped around and I kicked it away.

Greer ran to her people. "Come on. It's okay. Hunter Squad is here."

I waved them ahead of me, bringing up the rear. I kept my weapon up, watching the churning water. My squad was still firing on the creature.

Then suddenly, the final tentacle slipped back into the water.

The water went still.

Damn, I knew it wasn't dead. It was still in there. Waiting.

"Everyone inside," I yelled.

My squad mates nodded.

We followed Greer into the dam base.

CHAPTER FOUR

HUNTER SQUAD

Greer

I watched Jameson slam the base door closed. The howling wind was instantly silenced.

Adrenaline was pumping through my system, and I tried to calm my fast breathing. "Frankie, Jordan, are you both okay?"

They nodded, water dripping off their soaked clothes. Frankie was holding a hand to her head. Her dark, curly hair was a tangled mess around her face, and her usually dark skin had a pale tint. Jordan was middle-aged, bald, and built like a tank, but he looked shaken.

I saw the rest of the Hunter Squad step into view. Each and every one of them was tall, muscular, and clad in their high-tech armor.

"My arm..." Jordan held his arm up. "It's burning. The slime from that...thing, it burns."

I could see his skin was blistering.

"And it hurts like hell," he added.

"Frankie, get him down to the infirmary," I said,

The woman nodded. "I hit my head…I'm feeling a little…" She staggered.

"Frankie," I cried.

North lunged forward and caught her. She blinked up at him, then sagged, unconscious.

I pushed forward. "Is she all right?"

"She has a nasty lump on the back of her head." North frowned, his gloved hand gently probing Frankie's skull. "My guess is she has a concussion."

"Do you have a doctor here?" Jameson asked.

I shook my head. "We're well-stocked, but no medic."

North lifted Frankie into his arms. "I can help them."

Relief punched through me. "Thanks, North."

I watched Jordan lead North down the tunnel to the infirmary. I prayed Frankie would be okay.

Then a big, broad body stepped in front of me.

"You're bleeding." Jameson touched my cheek. "You have a cut over your eye."

I swiped at my wet hair. "It's nothing."

"It could get infected. I'll clean it for you."

"Here." One of my engineers rushed forward carrying a stack of towels. "So you can all dry off." He handed them out to the Hunter Squad soldiers.

I watched as Kai, Marc, and Zeke started toweling off their wet hair.

"Come on," I said to Jameson. "In my office."

I watched him swipe a towel over his brown hair as we walked down the bare-concrete corridor. I stopped at my office and pressed a palm to the lock. It pinged, and the door slid open.

Once inside, he pulled his chest armor off. He was wearing a black shirt beneath it. It was fitted and wet, and clung to him so tightly I could see the outline of his abs under the fabric.

God, don't look at his abs, Greer. I swallowed and blew out a breath. Then I reached up and touched my cut. "Ow."

"Sit." His voice was gruff.

I sat on the edge of my desk, shifting a stack of files. My office wasn't very big. There were large light panels on the wall to make up for the lack of natural light, and just my untidy desk and chair. My computer was lost in the files and schematics littering the surface.

"Sorry about the mess in here."

"It's fine. First aid kit?"

"In that cabinet."

He pulled it out and opened the kit, then crouched in front of me.

My heart did a wild flip in my chest. *It's Jameson. You're childhood friends. He's practically your brother.*

None of it worked. I was excruciatingly aware of him. There was no way I'd think of Jameson Steele as my brother.

He took out some gauze and poured some antiseptic onto it. Then he leaned in and gently wiped the cut.

"You shouldn't have been out there, Greer."

I blinked. "What?"

Steady hazel eyes met mine. For a second, I was lost in the green, counting the gold flecks I could see.

"When you see a giant monster, you run away. You don't run toward it."

I straightened. "I did my job. This is my worksite and my people. Those were *my* guys in danger. I'd already watched one man get dragged into the water." My voice cracked. God, I couldn't believe Sam and Travis were gone. "Everyone here is my responsibility, and I had to get Frankie and Jordan to safety."

"Not if it risks your own life."

A small laugh choked out of me. "I can't believe you said that. Considering what you do for a living. You risk your life every day."

His brow creased. "That's different. I'm trained."

I snorted. "So what? I wasn't going to let my people get eaten by that *thing*."

He put some cream on my cut, and I hissed.

"Sorry," he said.

Now, I sighed. "I wasn't being reckless, Jameson. But I had to help. I'm the lead engineer. This is my job. It's vital that we establish a secure water supply for the Sydney area. Our civilization depends on it."

"Getting yourself killed won't help anyone."

"Hey." I noted the tension in his body. His shoulders were taut, the muscles in his neck strained. He was worried. I cupped his strong jaw, my fingers brushing over his stubble. He was so big. So muscular and strong. "I'm all right. You and the squad arrived at the perfect time."

He gave a tight nod. Then he gently pressed a bandage over my cut. I swallowed. Who would have guessed such a big guy could be so gentle?

"No more fighting the monsters. That's my job."

I smiled. "Deal."

He was so close, and he smelled of rain with a hint of perspiration. I liked it. Desire flared hot and quick. I fought the urge to fidget. "I haven't seen you for ages. You haven't called, and you didn't return the messages I left."

He was quiet for a beat. "I've been busy. You've been busy."

I sensed it was more than that. "I always have time for you, Jameson."

He leaned closer, and I felt like the temperature in my office rose several degrees.

My fingers tightened on the edge of the desk. Was he going to kiss me? My heart thudded against my ribs.

There was the rap of knuckles on the door. "Dinner's ready."

I recognized Marc's voice.

"The engineers are cooking for everyone. Come and get it, or I'll eat it all."

Jameson leaned back, the moment evaporating. Intense disappointment flooded me.

He wasn't going to kiss me. He never looked at me like that. I might not think of him as a brother, but I was certain he thought of me as a sister.

Suddenly, I felt dejected. Everything that had happened today crashed in on top of me.

Jameson cleared his throat. "Once the weather clears, we'll send a drone out to check for the monster."

"Okay. I've seen a few ripples in the water the last few days. That's why I wanted to talk with you, but if I'd had any idea what we were facing..." God, maybe if I'd called Jameson earlier, Travis and Sam would still be alive.

He gripped my arm and squeezed. "You couldn't have known. That's the biggest problem with the monsters. They're all different, and we never know what to expect. We'll gather intel on this one, and then my squad and I will come up with a plan to kill it."

I licked my lips. "You're staying?"

"Yes." His brow creased. "I'm staying until that monster is dead. I'm *not* going to let it hurt you...or your team."

My throat tightened. "Thanks, Jameson."

He touched my jaw. The caress was brief, but I felt it everywhere. I felt his rough calluses, the strength of his touch. He was a soldier, a warrior. I knew he'd earned every one of those calluses.

"Come on." He took my hand and helped me off the desk. "You need to go and change out of those wet clothes."

I tried to keep my face friendly and casual and not show how much his touch affected me. "We have a small laundry. You and the guys can dry your gear."

He nodded. "Thanks. And don't worry, Greer. I'll keep you safe."

He'd keep my body safe, what about the rest of me? The part of me that liked having him close?

Jameson

I SHOVELED food into my mouth. The engineers had

done a good job. In our work, we burned a lot of calories, so any time someone cooked for us was good.

I glanced across the table at Greer. She'd changed into dry clothes, and I tried not to notice the way the soft, pink T-shirt hugged her breasts. She was nodding and eating as she listened to one of her engineers. Everyone was in a somber mood.

They were thinking of the people they'd lost. And Frankie in the infirmary, still unconscious. North had treated the woman, but she needed to be observed throughout the night. There was currently another engineer sitting with her. Everyone was hoping she woke up soon.

Greer patted one of her people on the back, smiling at them. She was so damn gorgeous. Her blonde hair didn't quite brush her shoulders and had a wave to it. It was shot through with strands of gold, honey, and pale sunshine.

Shit, I was no poet. Yet, here I was, obsessing over Greer's hair.

"Colbie landed in the ruins of the nearby town," Marc said. "She's got the Talon secured." He frowned. "She said she'd sleep in it."

"She isn't coming to the base?" Greer asked.

"The storm's too bad for her to get up here to the dam base," I said. "It's safer for her to stay with the Talon. Besides, we all know she'd never leave her beloved aircraft."

Marc's frown deepened. It wasn't a usual look for him, since he was the most easy-going of us. "What if something creeps up on her? She's alone. She could need help."

"Colbie can hold her own. You know that."

Marc pushed his chair back. "I'm going to call her on the comms and check on her." He strode off to the other side of the room.

"What's wrong with him?" I asked.

Kai shrugged.

A sudden echoing clang rang through the base. Everyone froze.

Clang.

Clang.

I slowly pushed to my feet, eyeing the walls.

Clang.

Clang.

"What the hell is that?" one of the engineers said, his voice shaky.

Clang.

This time, the sound was softer and farther along with dam wall.

"The monster's testing the wall," Zeke said.

Everyone gasped, then silence fell.

My jaw worked. This monster was not going to go down easily. "Let's check it out."

Greer rose. "I'm coming too."

I wanted to argue, but the stubborn look on her face warned me not to bother.

I strode down one of the tunnels, my squad behind me. Greer stayed at my side.

Clang.

We couldn't wait for the storm to clear. "We need to get a drone up and see what we're dealing with. North, Kai?"

The men nodded.

"On it," Kai said.

"You have a drone with you?" Greer asked.

I nodded. "Colbie dropped off some of our gear when she flew us in. The guys retrieved it earlier." We never went anywhere without extra weapons and ammunition.

A groove appeared in Greer's brow. "Isn't it too wet and windy for a drone to operate?"

"Calmer conditions would be better, but the drone's designed to work in bad weather. It's not ideal, but we'll see what we can see."

Kai and North reappeared, carrying a medium-size case from our gear. Kai flipped open the box and pulled out the high-tech quadcopter drone. Our tech guru, Maxim, liked to invent gadgets. He kept our armor enhanced, the Talon kitted out, and was always upgrading our weapons.

Kai and North headed for the exterior door. I heard a creak, followed by the howl of the wind.

I headed back to the long table where we'd eaten. Some of the engineers were still sitting there, looking worried.

I opened the tablet that controlled the drone. It was set in a rugged, tough casing. Marc and Zeke leaned against the wall, watching.

The screen flickered to life.

The drone flew up and I had a view of the dam wall. I spotted Kai and North, battered by the wind and rain, but staying close to the base door.

The drone moved over the dam, and the image was shaky. The wind was damn strong.

"It's too dark," Zeke said. "Visibility is shit."

I tapped my finger on the desk. *Where are you?*

There was a flash of movement in the water.

Greer leaned forward. *"There."*

Three tentacles burst out of the water.

"Fuck," Marc muttered.

I saw a glimpse of a large sucker mouth. Then the creature disappeared back into the water.

"We're going to die," one of the engineers whispered.

"No one's going to die," I growled. "Hunter Squad is going to do what we do best."

Marc nodded and folded his arms over his chest. "Turn that monster into mush."

"Okay, everyone, get to bed," Greer said. "It's been a rough night. The storm should clear by the morning, and we have work to do. It's what Travis and Sam would want. We won't let them have died in vain."

With nods, her team left and headed into the tunnels.

Kai and North returned. Both of them were wet again.

"You saw," Kai said.

"Yeah. It's big and ugly." I ran a hand through my hair. "I want two people on patrol. We'll have to cover being one man down. Kai and North, you take first shift, since you're already wet."

"Yay," North muttered. "Come on, Kaitoa. Let's babysit the monster."

"We'll find some rooms," Marc said, giving me a chin lift. "Get some shut eye."

With a nod, Zeke followed behind his brother.

That left me alone with Greer.

"You okay?" I asked.

She scrubbed a hand over her face. "Two people are dead. I should've anticipated this."

I gripped her shoulders. "How? We never know when the damn hybrids are going to appear. We all know the risks." We'd grown up knowing the monsters were out there.

She gave me a tired nod.

I pulled her close and hugged her. She pressed her face against my chest and held on tight.

Damn, that felt good. Too good.

I cleared my throat. "So, how are things with Toby?" I tried to keep my tone even and not show exactly how I felt about the douchebag.

She looked up. "You want to talk about my love life?"

"Just catching up."

"Well, Toby and I broke up over a month ago."

My pulse skipped. "Sorry."

"Don't be." She spun away. "That dinner we shared was horrible. I saw some of his true colors. And then, he told me that I needed to give up my work. So I could support his greatness."

I frowned. "What?"

"He decided I should be a stay-at-home mom and have lots of his babies. That his work was more important than mine."

My hand flexed. "I always thought he was an idiot."

She laughed. "Why didn't you ever tell me?"

"You seemed to like him, for some reason. I know that he was smart, with all his degrees."

"Well, I don't like him anymore, and I've sworn off

men. I have an important job to do. I don't need a man or sex getting in my way."

Hearing Greer say the word sex made my cock twitch. *Shit.* "Right."

She nodded. "Right." Then she sighed. "I'd better get to bed. I'll see you in the morning."

I nodded. "Good night, Greer."

She gave me a small smile. "Night, Jameson."

I stayed there for a long time, remembering how it felt to hold her. My hands flexed. Mostly, I tried not to think about the fact that she no longer belonged to someone else.

CHAPTER FIVE

Greer

I stepped out of the shower and toweled off my hair.

Now that I was back in my room, I wasn't tired. I was wired.

I was still worried about Frankie. I kept thinking of poor Travis and Sam. Travis had been a few years from retirement, and Sam had been young and full of potential. Grief hit and tears sprang into my eyes. I sank onto my bunk, fighting the pressure in my chest.

Those poor men. They must've been terrified.

I tried to push it out of my mind. I dressed in my favorite pink-striped pajama shorts and blue tank top, then moisturized my face and brushed my wet hair.

My thoughts turned to Jameson.

God, I needed to get a grip on this crush. My hand squeezed the handle of my brush.

But I knew it was more than a crush. It had been a crush when I was younger, but now I was a woman. I didn't just like his rough, tough looks. I liked his strength and his determination, that he was a good leader, and a loyal friend.

I bit my lip. Okay, maybe I liked his body too. All those muscles...

My mom was as tough as they came, and she said a fit, athletic man could easily make a smart woman lose her good sense.

She and my dad were disgustingly good together. They were always passionate, kissing and touching. I sighed. I wanted that. I wanted a guy to tear my clothes off and need me so much he couldn't hold back.

But the man I was most attracted to saw me as a sister.

He almost kissed you. At least, I *think* he almost had. There had definitely been a moment. I closed my eyes and imagined him right here, sitting beside me, touching me.

I lay back on the covers. Jameson would be rough, forceful in bed. He'd show me how he felt and what he wanted.

Sex with Toby had been decent. He'd talked a lot, and it hadn't always been sexy, but I'd come some of the time. But it had hardly been exciting or passionate.

With thoughts of Jameson still in my head, I reached over and opened the nightstand drawer. I pulled out my vibrator and shimmied my shorts and panties off.

If he was here, he'd run those callused hands over me. He'd touch every inch of my skin.

Tingles worked through my body, and I shivered. I turned on my vibrator. It was soundless. It was the latest model from my friend Hope's company. Her mom, Liberty, had started the company in the aftermath of the alien invasion. They'd started out making eco-friendly shampoos, conditioners, sunscreens and make-up, and then branched into vibrators and other toys.

I touched the toy between my legs and swallowed a moan. I imagined all the things Jameson would do to me. How his big body would feel against mine. His hands pinning me down.

I panted, my free hand gripping the sheets. I was getting close.

There was a knock on my door.

"Greer? I saw your light was on. Are you okay?"

Jameson.

God. With just the sound of his voice, I came. I rolled into my pillow to muffle my cries. Pleasure rolled through me in waves.

"Greer?"

"Coming." In more ways than one.

I shoved the vibrator in the drawer and yanked my panties and shorts up. My panties were soaked in an instant. *Oh boy.* Pleasure was still humming through me as I sat up.

Swallowing, I raked a hand through my hair and headed for the door. My knees felt weak.

Dragging in a deep breath, I pressed the door lock. The door slid open.

And there he was, filling the door frame with his big, muscular body. He was wearing cargo pants and a black T-shirt.

I felt another pull low in my belly.

He cocked his head. "Are you all right?"

"Fine. I'm fine. *Totally* fine."

His brow creased. "Your face is flushed. Are you sick?"

"No." God, I was about to die from embarrassment. I couldn't tell him that I'd just orgasmed, thinking of him. "Still warm from the shower." I realized he was carrying two steaming mugs.

"You're not okay. I knew you'd worry about Frankie, and about the guys you lost. I brought you hot chocolate. Your favorite."

I smiled and waved a hand for him to enter. "You know me too well."

He walked in and handed me a mug. He took a chair while I sat on the bed. He made my quarters seem tiny.

"I do know your weakness for chocolate," he said.

"I haven't seen much of you lately." I sipped. Mmm, the chocolate was so good. "Maybe I'd gotten over my chocolate obsession."

He shrugged a shoulder. "We've both been busy, and I knew you had a boyfriend taking up the rest of your time." The corner of his lips twitched. "I don't think you'll ever get over your chocolate obsession."

I reached out and touched his knee. "I know we've been busy with work, but I always have time for my friends."

An unreadable look crossed his face. "Friends. Always." He nodded at the mug. "Drink your chocolate."

I leaned back and moaned. "It's so good. Thank you." I looked up and froze.

The look on his face… His gaze was locked on my lips.

Pure heat hit my belly. "*Jameson?*" I whispered.

He jolted, then quickly sipped his own drink. "I just wanted to come and tell you that the guys you lost, it's not your fault. You're not to blame. The monster is the one at fault."

I sighed. "Logically, I know that. My heart just hasn't caught up yet. And I'm really worried about Frankie. She's a good friend."

He took my hand. "North is the best. He should be a practicing doctor, not on Hunter Squad."

"He loves Hunter Squad. He loves being a doctor, but he also loves being a soldier."

Jameson nodded.

"Poor Travis and Sam." Tears welled again and I dashed them away. "Sorry, I don't usually cry."

"Hey." He reached out and set our drinks down. Then he pulled me onto his lap.

He was so warm, and I pressed my face to his strong neck. I wanted to absorb him. How long had it been since someone had held me like this? Toby certainly hadn't.

"I've got you, Greer." His big hand ran up my back.

The tears fell and I leaned into him. I cried quietly, letting all the fear and grief out.

Thankfully, the crying jag didn't last long. Soon, I was just aware of him. Hot and hard beneath me.

I lifted my head. "Sorry about that."

"Nothing to be sorry about." His voice was gruff. His green-gold gaze was blazing as he looked at me.

"Jameson…"

I felt the connection arc between us. My breath hitched. God, I could see that he felt it, too.

He cupped my cheek—

A communicator pinged, and we both jolted.

"That's mine." Shaking my head to clear it, I grabbed my comm unit off the nightstand and read the message. "Oh." My heart surged. "Frankie is awake."

Jameson

I'D ALMOST KISSED HER.

I was a jerk.

Greer had been crying, worried. And I'd been turned on.

We were heading to the infirmary. I followed her down the tunnel. She'd pulled a sweater on over her tank top, thank God, but there were still miles of toned, bare legs on display.

I ground my teeth together.

I was *not* supposed to be drooling over her.

"God, I hope Frankie's okay," Greer murmured, fiddling with her damp hair. It looked shades darker than her usual blonde.

"I told you North would help her."

She nodded and shot me a small smile.

We reached the room they used as the infirmary. As the door whispered open, I saw North standing by a bunk. Frankie looked pale against the sheets, her curly, dark hair all tangled.

"*Frankie.*" Greer hurried forward and took her friend's hand.

"Hey, there." The woman sounded woozy.

"How are you doing?" Greer asked.

"Well, the last thing I remember is a huge, ugly monster. Then I woke up and saw a hot doctor." She fluttered her lashes in North's direction.

Greer laughed. "You're definitely feeling better. And North is very easy on the eyes."

I frowned. She thought North was handsome?

Damn. He was. We gave him hell about it. I'd never had a problem catching the attention of the ladies, but I knew I wasn't pretty. I scraped a hand over my jaw.

"Is the monster dead?" Frankie asked. "I don't really remember much. It's all hazy." She shuddered.

Greer's mouth flattened. "No, it's not dead."

"But it will be." I stepped forward. "Soon."

Frankie smiled at me. "Hi, Jameson."

"Hi."

"I bet Greer was glad to see you."

"I was," Greer said hurriedly. "Glad that Hunter Squad was here to deal with the monster."

"Is Jordan okay?" Frankie asked.

"Just some minor contact burns," North answered.

Frankie sat up a little higher. "And Travis and Sam?"

Greer's face fell. She shook her head.

"Oh, God." Frankie pressed a shaky hand to her mouth.

"We're going to get the dam project up and running." Greer's voice was firm. "In their honor."

Frankie nodded. "It's what they would've wanted."

As the women continued to talk, I moved over to North. "How's she doing?"

"She has a nasty concussion, but she'll be all right. She needs rest."

"Good work."

North nodded. "All right, Greer. Frankie needs to rest."

"So does Greer," I added.

She smiled at her friend. "I'll stop in and see you in the morning."

"Bring me coffee," Frankie said with a pleading look.

I followed Greer out of the infirmary. Halfway down the tunnel, she stopped.

I frowned at her. "Greer?"

She held up a hand. "I've already lost it once tonight. I don't want to make it a second time. I'm just glad she's okay."

The welling tears in her blue eyes made me feel like dirt. "You can lose it as many times as you want." I pulled her close.

She pressed her face to my chest. She felt so damn good in my arms.

She held on tightly. There was no sobbing this time, just silent tears that soaked into my shirt.

"I'm so glad Frankie will be fine. And so sad Travis and Sam aren't."

"It's going to be all right." I tipped her face up, brushing my thumbs across her cheeks. I liked that she was on the tall side, and I didn't have to bend too far.

"You must think I'm weak."

"Hardly. You're a kickass engineer who likes to get

her hands dirty, and takes care of her team. Caring doesn't make you weak, Greer."

She managed a smile. "You make me feel better. Thanks. It seems you can carry anything on these broad shoulders of yours."

I'd carry anything for her. I cupped her shoulders. "I'm always here for you."

The air between us changed. Charged. Like it had earlier between us back in her quarters. She stepped closer and I felt the tantalizing brush of her breasts against my chest.

Damn. My cock hardened.

"Jameson." Her voice was low and sexy.

Everything about her was sexy.

"Greer..." I cupped her jaw.

Then we both moved. I lowered my head as she went up on her toes. Her lips pressed to mine.

With a groan, I pulled her against me. She shimmied closer and I plunged my tongue into her sweet mouth.

Her tongue touched mine, stroked. She tasted like every fantasy I'd ever had. She moaned into my mouth, her hands twisting in my shirt. Then she leaped up, her legs wrapping around my waist. I slid my hands under her ass, turned, and pinned her to the concrete wall.

Then I stopped holding back.

I devoured her. I kissed her with all the pent-up desire I'd had simmering for years. I kissed her until her lips were pliant and puffy under mine. I moved my mouth down the side of her neck. She undulated against me, rubbing that sweet pussy against me. I was as hard as steel.

"Jameson... *God*..."

Greer. This was Greer. We'd grown up together.

I shouldn't be doing this.

I let her go and staggered back.

She pressed a hand to the wall, and another to her swollen lips. She frowned at me.

I'd been rough. She was too good and smart for me. She was family.

"I'm sorry. I shouldn't have done that." I scraped a hand over my head. "I'm sorry."

"Jameson—"

I spun and hurried away, my boots echoing on the concrete floor.

I needed to find some damn control. I needed to focus on hunting this monster.

I had a job to do, and it didn't involve kissing Greer Baird.

CHAPTER SIX

Greer

With my hands on my hips, I stood on the dam wall, watching my team work.

Sunshine filled the morning, as if the storm had never happened. My chest squeezed. But we all knew that Travis and Sam were gone. A pall hung over the worksite.

I let out a breath and my gaze moved to the water. Today, it was as smooth as glass. Not a single ripple.

There had been no sign of the monster so far, and I hoped it stayed that way.

My gaze shifted. North and Zeke stood nearby, carbines resting in their arms. They were watching the water with a scary intensity while they murmured to each other. Keeping my team safe.

Jameson was inside with Marc and Kai. They were planning how to take down the monster.

Jameson. That kiss.

It was all I could think about. I'd slept like crap. Yes, a

part of it was because of grief and worry, and a part of it because of that kiss. It had been more than I'd imagined. Hot, fierce, passionate. And I'd imagined a lot when it came to Jameson. I touched my lips.

The kiss had been incredible.

Then he'd backed away like I was a monster.

I sighed and rubbed my forehead. *Focus on your job, Greer.*

I'd been to see Frankie in the infirmary. She was doing better. Too busy flirting with North to apparently be concerned about her health. I smiled. Frankie loved to flirt.

She'd teased me about Jameson, since she was well-versed on my crush. But today, I wasn't in the mood.

He'd rejected me.

And it hurt.

Hell, it hurt more than breaking up with Toby. He'd never understood me, or my need to work.

Jameson did, but he clearly didn't want me the same way I wanted him.

"Greer?"

The female voice made me turn. I spotted a short, slim redhead heading my way. She wore dark cargo pants and an olive-green T-shirt, and walked with a brisk stride, like she was in a rush. She'd walked like that when she'd been a little girl too.

I grinned. "Hey, Colbie."

We hugged. The light shone off her brilliant-red hair. She was tiny, compared to me. I always thought she looked like a sweet, delicate fairy, but she could drink most of the guys under the table. She also had a big laugh and a strong personality. No one got the better of Colbie Erickson.

"Were you okay last night?" I asked. "Sleeping in the quadcopter?"

"Yep. The Talon and I bedded down in town."

I'd been into the old town of Warragamba. There wasn't much left. "The ruins are kinda spooky."

Both of us glanced toward the wreckage of Warragamba. I knew that it had once been a bustling little place before the invasion.

"Thanks to Maxim, the Talon has a wicked security system," Colbie said. "If a fly even touches it, *bam*, it gets zapped with a gazillion volts."

I laughed. "Deadly."

"Yeah, I love my Talon. Sleek, sexy, dangerous. Better than a guy. And less annoying."

"How are you doing, hanging with Hunter Squad?"

"Great. I keep them in line." Then Colbie's face turned serious. "We do important work. Doing our bit to keep the world safe."

I nodded. I understood that and I'd gotten a firsthand look at it yesterday.

Colbie bounced a little, turning to look at the dam wall. "And you're going to keep us in clean drinking water."

"That's the plan. If we can solve our monster problem."

"Oh, Jameson will sort out the monster." Colbie waved a hand. "That's what he's good at."

"Yeah." I tucked my hair behind my ear, once again thinking of that kiss.

Colbie's gaze narrowed. "Are you blushing?"

"I don't blush. Have you met my mom? Claudia Baird does not blush, nor does her daughter."

Colbie stroked her chin. "I'm sensing something. Reminds me of that time we stole those cupcakes from your mom's kitchen, snuck into the backyard, and ate them all."

"We were six."

"Your mom busted us, and you had the same look on your face."

I bit my lip. "I..."

"Don't lie to me, girlfriend."

"Jameson and I kissed." The words rushed out of me.

"*Oh.*" Colbie's eyes went wide. "*Finally.*"

I frowned. "What do you mean finally?"

The pilot waved a hand. "Go on. Tell me everything."

"We kissed. He pinned me to the wall."

"Oh, boy." Colbie fanned herself. "Keep going. I haven't had sex in so long, and this is as close as I've come."

"It was amazing."

"I figured it would be. Jameson's just got this focus, you know? And all those muscles."

I frowned. I wasn't sure I liked Colbie noticing Jameson's muscles.

"Don't leave me hanging, Greer."

"He kissed me, then... He pulled away like I was toxic, and he apologized."

Colbie winced. "Not the ending I was hoping for."

I sighed. "Me neither."

She touched my arm. "Girl, he's a leader. So, he's big into responsibility. He sacrifices his own needs for the good of others every day. Both his squad and the people he saves. Plus, you two grew up together. He feels a family obligation. And, he's probably worried your father will get out his sniper rifle."

I gave her a sad smile. "If he really wanted me, if he really felt something, nothing would stop him." I straightened my shoulders. "Anyway, enough of this. I want a guy who is crazy about me. Who'll jump through fire for me, no compromising."

Colbie's lips quirked and she nodded. "Hell, yeah. We all deserve that."

"Now, I'm going to check in and see what plans they have for this monster."

"I'll join you."

We headed inside. I felt better after our little chat. Focused. Work was all I needed to care about right now.

The air was cooler in the base and goosebumps pimpled my skin. We turned a corner, and my gaze instantly snapped to Jameson. He was leaning over a table, and wearing a black shirt that clung to his muscled chest.

My insides felt like they'd been hit by a blowtorch. His short sleeves displayed his huge biceps in all their glory. My belly fluttered.

Oh, man.

Beside me, Colbie giggled. "Girl, you are in trouble."

"Shut up." I raised my voice. "How's it coming?"

Jameson's head jerked up and his hazel gaze locked on me. I kept my face friendly and professional.

Or at least, I hoped I did.

"We have some ideas." Marc's gaze locked on Colbie. "Hey, sparrow."

She pulled a face. "Don't call me that."

"But you're as cute as a sparrow and you like to fly."

I hid my laugh at Colbie's disgruntled face. "So, you have a plan?" I wanted to change the subject before Colbie committed an act of violence.

"Our best idea is to kill it," Marc said.

"Brilliant," Colbie said. "How long did it take you to come up with that plan?"

"Shut it, little sparrow." He winked at her. "I suggested we blow it up."

"No," I said. "That will contaminate the water."

"That's what the boss man said, too."

I looked at Jameson. "You have a better idea?"

He nodded. "Electrocute it."

Colbie nodded slowly. "Nice."

"We need Maxim," Jameson said.

Maxim Ivanov had a genius IQ, and kept Hunter Squad in gadgets and tech. I knew he also helped out our engineers here and there on different projects, when we needed his expertise.

If anyone could come up with something to electrocute a giant monster, it was him.

"Sasha, did you get all of that?" Jameson said. "Can you tell Maxim to have his gear ready?"

I couldn't hear the comms officer's response, but then Jameson nodded and looked at his pilot.

"Colbie, can you go and get him?"

She tossed him a salute. "Yes, boss."

Jameson

I WALKED along the dam wall, my gaze on the water.

A few birds arrowed down, diving for fish, before flying back into the sky. Nothing was concerning them, but I knew the monster wouldn't be far away. It was intent on attacking the dam wall and eating the workers.

Greer's team was working on the wall, but staying as far from the water as possible. Several of them were wearing exo-suits, lifting blocks into place to reinforce the wall, but I found her instantly. The sunlight gleamed off her hair. She was talking to one of her guys. Then she smiled and laughed.

My gut clenched.

She'd been ignoring me today. Giving me polite looks, or sometimes looking right through me.

It's your own damn fault.

I'd kissed her. Devoured her.

I should never have touched her. If Uncle Shaw found out… Worse, if Aunt Claudia found out…

My hand flexed. I walked to the far end of the wall, my carbine slung over my shoulder, ready if I needed it.

I had to keep my hands off Greer.

But I couldn't stop reliving that damn kiss. The feel of her pinned between me and the wall, her sweet body rubbing against mine.

"You're deep in thought."

Kai's voice made me jerk. Damn, the man could be

quiet when he wanted to be. "Thinking about the monster."

He made a sound. "Thinking about monsters makes you hard?"

I glanced down at the tented front of my cargo pants. I growled. "Why are you checking out my junk?"

"I wasn't. I'm just observant." Kai ran his tongue over his teeth. "My guess is you're thinking about Greer."

I speared my friend with a look.

"If you think how you feel about her is a secret, you're sorely mistaken, my friend."

Heaving out a breath, I shoved a hand through my hair. "It'll pass."

Kai snorted. "You've been pining for her for years."

"I have not."

"Jameson, Greer is awesome. Smart, attractive...ask her out."

I looked back at the water. "We kissed."

"Finally."

I shook my head. "No. She's family. I'm older than her and I'm not smart enough for her. She deserves—"

"That's bullshit, Jameson. Some of those things you need to navigate, but it doesn't make anything impossible. And you're plenty smart. Best squad leader I've ever served with."

"He's right."

When Sasha's voice joined in via my earpiece, I rolled my eyes to the sky. "This is not up for discussion."

"If you like her, show her," Sasha said. "Show her that she's worth it."

"I kissed her, then I apologized. It's not happening again."

Sasha groaned. "You're an idiot."

I scowled. "Just drop it, you two." I touched my earpiece and cut Sasha's feed.

Kai held up his hands. "All right. Go back to the pining."

"Can you go and check on North?" I growled.

"Fine."

I stayed there, staring blindly at the water and trees. Greer wasn't for me.

Splash.

I spun, muscles tensing. I saw ripples in the water. Maybe it had just been a fish?

No. My gut was telling me our unwanted friend was back. I scanned across the dam and spotted movement.

"Everyone back from the water," I bellowed.

Greer and the others jolted, then scrambled away.

A tentacle rose up. I whipped my carbine up. A second later, Zeke was beside me.

The tentacle crept out onto the dam wall, feeling its way along the concrete.

"Jameson?" Zeke murmured.

"Don't fire yet." I touched my ear. "Sasha, we have contact with the monster. Tell Kai to get the drone in the air. I want you monitoring the feed."

"On it, J," she replied.

A moment later, I heard the whirr of the drone as it whipped by overhead. The creature was swimming along the wall.

"It's just...looking," Zeke said.

It was after something.

I got the feeling it was smarter than we gave it credit for. I'd learned never to underestimate the monsters. Some were mindless and ravenous, others... Others were smart and cunning.

"What's it doing?" Greer's voice behind me.

"I'm not sure. It's just looking around."

"Why?"

"We're going to find out. Stay behind me."

"Well, I wasn't going to take a swim," she said tartly.

Zeke snorted, and I shot him a look.

More ripples appeared in the water.

"It's leaving," Zeke said.

It was swimming away from the dam wall. I walked to the edge of the wall. It was moving fast and picking up speed.

I turned and ran along toward the far end of the wall, heading to the far bank. I leaped off and onto the grass. Zeke was right behind me.

"Let's see where it goes."

He nodded and followed.

I touched my ear. "Kai, Zeke and I will see where this thing is going. Keep an eye on the dam."

"Acknowledged," Kai said over the comm line.

Then Greer leaped off the wall as well.

I frowned at her and held up a hand. "You stay here."

She lifted her chin. "No, I'm coming." She marched forward, and that's when I saw her hand on the blaster holstered on her belt.

Damn, she was stubborn. I knew there was no point

in arguing. "Then stay between Zeke and me. No arguments."

She looked like she wanted to argue, but finally she nodded.

The three of us set off through the trees, sticking to the edge of the water. I could see the bulk of the monster just beneath the surface. *Where was it going? Did it have a lair nearby?*

Then it sank down into the water and out of sight

"Dammit."

"Jameson." Sasha's voice in my earpiece. "I still have a visual. It's continuing along in the water, about three hundred meters ahead of you."

I nodded at the others and broke into a jog. "Come on."

The trees were lush, and the birds in the trees were singing. I breathed in, pulling in the fresh scent of eucalyptus. I tried to imagine what the bush had been like before the invasion. When you could go hiking without fear of monsters.

"It stopped," Sasha said. "I've lost sight of it. It's right near the bank, and the trees are too thick. I think it might have left the water. I'm not sure what it's doing."

"Acknowledged."

We kept running. Zeke moved silently—the guy could move like a ghost. Greer wasn't silent, but she was managing to keep up.

The trees thinned out and the water came back into view. We were just in time to see tentacles sliding back into the water.

"It's gone," Greer said.

On the shore was a large patch of flattened grass and some crushed wildflowers.

"It came out of the water." Zeke walked forward, frowning.

Suddenly a tentacle speared out of the water, aiming for us.

In an instant, Zeke and I had our carbines up. We fired.

The tentacle went wild, trying to dodge the laser fire, then slid back into the water.

"Jameson, I see it now," Sasha said. "It's moving away from your location."

I blew out a breath, spotting the drone arrowing out across the dam. "Thanks, Sash." I looked at the others. "It's gone." I walked over to where it had been lying.

Why the hell had it come on to land? "I have no idea what it was doing."

"Maybe it attacked an animal?" Greer suggested.

Zeke crouched, touching the grass. "Jameson."

I walked over, and what I saw made my gut clench.

"What is it?" Greer's arm brushed mine.

I had to fight to lock down the sensation. "Footprints." I pointed.

The footprints were clearly made by monsters with five claws on their toes.

Ones that walked upright.

"Monster prints." Her brow creased. "I don't understand."

A cold feeling seeped into my chest. "The aquatic monster met other monsters here."

Her mouth dropped open. "No. That can't be right."

I glanced at the water. "The monsters were meeting."

CHAPTER SEVEN

HUNTER SQUAD

Greer

Fighting off my general feeling of disquiet, I focused on working on my tablet. I was sitting in the shade on the dam wall, my team working, and Hunter Squad on security detail.

There'd been no sign of the monster since this morning. I nibbled my lip, filled with edgy worry. The monster shouldn't have been meeting with other monsters. I still couldn't believe it. They weren't that smart, and they couldn't communicate with each other. They didn't work together. They were just hungry, wild, mutated beasts.

I'd heard stories of the Gizzida growing up. The alien species had been smart. Dad loved to tell us about all the fights Hell Squad and the berserkers had gotten into. My parents were heroes. They'd helped save the world.

I'd also heard plenty of stories of the hybrid monsters left behind, as well. But by all accounts, most were singular and solitary. The presumption had been they weren't clever, just mindless killing beasts. We'd never seen any evidence about them being smart enough to work as a group.

If they were working together now...

No. An icy shiver skated down my spine. Hunter Squad would kill this monster, end of story. I'd get this project finished and the dam operational.

I looked at my team. They were all still reeling from the loss of Travis and Sam, but they were doing their jobs.

There was a whoosh of sound above, and I looked up. The Talon stopped in the air, hovering, then I watched as it lowered onto a grassy area nearby.

It looked like Colbie was back with Maxim.

I glanced at the dam plans again. There were some tweaks I wanted to make to the design. I'd get Frankie and Jordan to check it over with me. As I tucked the tablet away, I saw Jameson walking my way and my heart knocked against my ribs. Why did he affect me like this? I just wanted to keep looking at him.

Fighting the urge to tug at my clothes, I rose and straightened my shoulders. Jameson Steele was *not* my focus.

He would never be mine.

Ignoring the shot of pain from that thought, I turned to face him. His gaze met mine, and I shot him a breezy smile.

His brows drew together.

"I'm back." Colbie walked over to us, bouncing as always.

Right behind her came a handsome, dark-haired man. Maxim was tall and lean, his dark hair a little long. He looked like he should be a pirate marauder, or a spy, or something else, dark and ruthless. Someone who worked in the shadows.

He saw me and smiled. "Greer." He lifted me off my feet and smacked a kiss to my lips. "Beautiful as always."

I rested my hands on his shoulders. "And you're as charming as ever."

"Maxim, we have work to do." Jameson's terse voice.

"There's always time to kiss a beautiful woman, my friend." Maxim shot me a wink. "Especially a smart one."

I couldn't help but smile back. His harmless flirting felt nice.

Behind me, Jameson growled. I glanced back and frowned at him.

"We have a monster to kill," he said.

Maxim nodded and set me down. "Show me what we're dealing with."

We walked across the dam wall to where Kai was standing, surveilling the water.

"We haven't seen the asshole for a while." Kai crossed his arms over his chest.

"It's there," Jameson murmured. "Lurking." Then, he pointed across the water.

In the center of the dam, a tiny ripple suddenly bubbled. We waited, and for a full minute, nothing happened. Kai picked up a rock and flung it. It sailed through the air, then landed with a splash.

Four tentacles peeked out of the water.

"Hmm. It looks big." Maxim's gaze narrowed. "Sasha said you want to electrocute it?"

"I don't want to contaminate the water," I said. "We have good filtration systems, but…"

Maxim nodded. "Understood. Monsters are filled with nasties." He stroked his jaw. "I can devise something to electrocute it."

"Good," Jameson said. "Get to work."

Maxim jerked his head. "Kai, help me bring my gear from the Talon."

"There's a lot of it," Colbie warned.

"A genius needs his tools," Maxim quipped.

"We have a decent-size workshop you can use," I said. "It's all yours. It has a roller door to the outside on the far end of the dam. I'll go and open it for you."

"Perfect," Maxim said.

I watched Maxim, Colbie, and Kai head back to the Talon. They started pulling crates and bags out of the quadcopter's cargo hold. I headed for the workshop, put the code into the lock, and the large roller door slowly rumbled open.

"This should do," Jameson said.

I jolted at the sound of his voice. I hadn't heard him follow me.

"The quicker Maxim gets this done, the quicker my team can get back to work." I shifted some stuff on one of the workbenches, stacking it to one side.

Jameson sighed. "Greer—"

Maxim stepped inside, his lean body silhouetted by the sunlight. He looked around at the workbenches and nodded. "Good." He set a toolbox down and barked orders at the others carrying in his equipment.

It wasn't long before he was setting his gear up and

plugging in several devices. Soon, he got lost in his work. I knew from experience that once Maxim was in the zone, nothing else existed for him.

I got it. I felt the same way about my work.

That's exactly how I wanted a man to feel about me. Like nothing else existed.

My parents had a love like that. They often fought—sometimes spectacularly—but they made up just as passionately. Dad had risked everything to rescue my mom during the invasion.

I wouldn't settle for anything less.

I glanced at Jameson. His back was to me, and for a moment, I greedily took in the slabs of muscle. Then I made myself turn away and head back to my team.

"Jordan, come and see the changes I want to make to the design."

Jameson

I STOPPED IN THE DOORWAY, watching Maxim work. The man stood at a bench, with metal wires and electrodes and who-knew-what lying in front of him.

He hadn't heard me. I shook my head. Maxim was well-trained and could fight, but this was his true passion.

Turning, I looked out the open roller door. My gaze glanced over Greer's people. Everything had been quiet this afternoon.

Too quiet.

I spotted Greer. Again, she was ignoring me.

I slid a hand into my pocket. I hated this tension between us. I wanted her to smile at me.

When Maxim had kissed her earlier, I'd almost lost my shit. I knew it had just been friendly, but I didn't want any other man's lips on hers. I blew out a breath.

I had to stop thinking about her.

Kai walked over to me and gave me a chin lift.

"Everything okay?" I asked.

"No sign of our friend."

"It's not far away." I could feel it close by. Skulking. "Any luck with the prints from the monsters it met with?" I'd sent Kai and Zeke out to see if they could find the other monsters.

Kai shook his head. "I tracked them into the forest, but the ground got too dry, and I lost them."

He was the best tracker I'd ever seen. He had an uncanny ability to read tracks and signs, to sense things. An ability he'd no doubt inherited from his alien mother. Selena Rahia's species had been the enemies of the Gizzida and she'd been taken prisoner. Kai's father, Tane, had rescued her and they'd fallen in love.

Selena had all kinds of amazing skills, all linked to nature. While Kai and his sister hadn't inherited all of their mother's abilities, they still had ingrained skills I knew had to have come from their mom.

If Kai couldn't track the monsters, no one could.

"Okay, keep me posted. I'm going to check on Maxim." I strode inside the workshop, my eyes adjusting to the lower light. We needed this weapon. The sooner the monster was dead, the sooner we got out of here.

Away from the temptation of Greer Baird.

"Maxim? Maxim?" Nothing. His dark head stayed bent over some metal and wires.

I thumped my fist against the workbench.

His head jerked up, annoyance on his face. He had a small device over one eye, which I guessed was filled with specs and info.

"What?" His voice was terse and grumpy.

"How's it going?"

He turned off the small multitool in his hand. "It would go faster if you didn't disturb me."

I was used to Maxim's temperamental moods. "I need an update."

My friend flicked up the eyepiece. "Fine. It's coming along." He pointed to a metallic, spherical device about the size of a basketball, resting on a stand on the workbench.

I frowned. "It'll generate enough power to fry our monster?"

"Yes." Maxim's gaze slid away from mine.

I sighed. "What's the catch?"

"It needs to be inside the creature for maximum effect."

My mouth flattened. "Inside? We need to get it to swallow it?"

"Yes."

"Jeez, Maxim, that won't be easy."

He shrugged. "That's your job. I'll design it, you find a way to get it inside the creature."

I rubbed my brow, feeling a headache forming. "Fine. When will it be ready?"

He leaned against the bench, crossed his arms, and narrowed his gaze. "In a rush to get home?"

"Yeah, something like that."

"Why?"

"Because."

"Anything to do with our delectable head engineer?"

I took a step forward. "Why are you calling her delectable?" I barely held back a growl.

"Because she is." He gave me a shit-eating grin. "And because it annoys you."

I wanted to hit him. "Get back to work."

"Why don't you tell her how you feel?"

I stiffened.

"You're pining for her—"

"I'm not pining." Fuck, why did everyone keep telling me that? "Just focus on the job, Maxim."

"You have feelings for her."

He wasn't going to drop it. I blew out a breath. "She's smart and gorgeous and going places. I'm just a grunt."

Maxim frowned. "You don't think you're good enough for her?"

I shrugged a shoulder. "She deserves the best. And anything between us would risk a family mess."

"She does deserve the best, Jameson. She deserves a good, honest man who'll love and protect her. Who'll put her first."

"Just get back to work." I turned to leave.

"Jameson?"

I paused, my fists clenching, but I didn't look back.

"She watches you back."

Heaving in a breath, I walked out, but Maxim's words were like a punch to my gut.

Did she? She'd sure as hell kissed me back. Kissed me with a hungry desire that still had my gut tight and my cock half hard. I shook my head. Evening was falling and I had a job to do.

"Listen up," I said, raising my voice. "Everyone needs to finish up now. I don't want anyone out here after dark."

There were nods, and I watched as some of Greer's team started packing their tools and gear away.

Greer appeared. Her face was set in blank lines. Like she was about to talk to a stranger. "Dinner will be ready soon. Colbie and a few of my guys are cooking up a feast. Something to try and keep everyone's spirits up."

"Sounds good. I want everyone inside soon."

She nodded.

"Maxim's making progress. The electro device will be ready tomorrow."

"So soon?"

"Yeah. Hopefully, your monster will be dead tomorrow, and we'll be out of your hair."

She clenched her hands together. "Sounds like you can't wait to get away from here."

I frowned. "That's not it. I thought you'd be happy to have the situation resolved."

She pasted a smile on. "Of course, I will."

Something inside me snapped. "Enough with the fake smiles, Greer."

"It's the only smile you're getting." She spun.

I grabbed her arm. "Hang on. I apologized for the kiss. I was out of line."

She jerked her arm away and spun back to face me. Her face was furious. "I didn't want a stupid apology."

My chest felt tight. I hated seeing her upset. "I hate this distance between us. You're important to me, Greer."

A spasm crossed her face. "Just not important enough." She looked away and her shoulders sagged. "Just go, Jameson."

"No." I took a step closer. "I shouldn't have touched you, shouldn't have kissed you—"

She made an angry sound and gripped the front of my shirt. "I wanted you to kiss me, you big oaf. I've wanted it for a long time."

My brain stopped working. *What?*

She shook her head, went up on her toes, and kissed me.

I didn't think, I just reacted. I hauled her close and kissed her back.

She made a hungry sound, and the kiss turned fierce. We attacked each other. I loved the taste of her, loved the sounds of her moans.

Then she pulled back.

We were both panting.

"That's what I wanted," she said breathily. "Not a damn apology."

What the hell?

Then she turned and stalked away.

CHAPTER EIGHT

HUNTER SQUAD

Greer

Dinner was a fun, noisy affair.

Maxim had a sexy laugh, and my female engineers were drooling over him. Everyone was enjoying the food, and letting off some of the tension of a dangerous situation, and the grief over our lost friends.

It was something my mom and dad had always told me. You had to grieve, but also make the most of the good times. You had to hang onto all the good you had in your life. That it helped you survive the bad times. I guess the alien invasion had taught them that.

Colbie and some of my engineers had cooked up some great dishes. I'd gorged myself on an amazing lentil curry and some of Colbie's famous spiced chicken wings. Frankie had been given the all-clear by North and had joined us. She was on light duties for another two weeks.

Across the table Marc chuckled, long and loud, at something Frankie had said. He'd always been louder and more easy-going than his twin. Zeke was more like his dad Gabe—quiet, intense, brooding.

Speaking of brooding.

Jameson sat at the head of the table. He'd been quiet all night, and I'd felt him watching me several times. I glanced over at him.

Oh. He was looking at me now, his hands steepled under his chin. I crossed my legs. His gaze felt like a touch. I wished I knew what he was thinking.

Our second kiss had been on replay in my head all evening. I was pretty sure he now knew that I didn't think of him as a brother or cousin, or any other sort of relative.

I got that our family was a factor. A messy breakup would cause problems.

But life was messy, especially in the aftermath of an alien invasion. And sometimes, things were worth the risk.

"All right, everyone, listen up," Jameson said. The sounds and conversations died down as everyone turned to look at him.

"Maxim says the device will be ready to launch tomorrow."

The table went even quieter.

"My squad and I have a plan to get the device close to the monster. Hopefully, by this time tomorrow, it'll be dead, and we'll have justice for your friends. And then you can get your project completed."

"Yes!" one engineer said.

Others nodded and cheers broke out.

Jameson held up a hand. "It's not done yet. Plan your

celebration for *after* the monster's dead." His gaze touched mine. "My squad will be on patrol shifts tonight. I want everyone to get a good night's sleep."

With a nod, he stood and left. Slowly, people started to drift out.

After checking in with a few of my engineers, I headed for my room. I was too wired to sleep. Would the device work? I gnawed on my bottom lip. Could Hunter Squad take down the monster?

What if someone else got hurt or killed?

No. Hunter Squad could do this. There was no doubt about that. They'd been keeping us safe for years. Jameson had taken over Hunter Squad several years ago, and little kids grew up knowing the squad would protect them.

I took a quick shower and put on my pajamas. I tried to read for a bit.

Nope, still too wired. I set my tablet down. There was going to be no sleep for me anytime soon. I remembered that the hot chocolate the other night had helped. I slipped out of my quarters and headed for the kitchen.

The base was silent and dark, everyone in bed and sleeping. I knew that some of Hunter Squad would be outside doing the rounds.

At least the monster wasn't banging on the wall again.

Tomorrow, we'd eliminate it. That was all I needed to focus on.

In the kitchen, I opened the fridge. The glow of light was like a beacon in the darkness. I grabbed some milk and hot chocolate powder and put it on the heat unit.

A moment later it dinged, and I poured the cocoa into a mug.

"Hey."

I jolted and turned. "You nearly gave me a heart attack. Make some more noise when you sneak up on a girl next time."

Jameson stood there, mostly hidden in the darkness. Then he reached up and pulled his armored vest off.

"You were outside?" I asked.

"Just finished patrol. Kai took over."

"The monster?"

"No sign of it."

"Good." I sipped my drink.

"Couldn't sleep?"

"No." I circled the counter and saw his gaze drop to my bare legs. His jaw tightened. "Jameson?"

"It's going to be okay. I don't want you to worry."

"I can't just turn the worry off." I leaned against the island and sipped again. "I know that you and your squad are good. And you always keep your promises. Like your dad. My mom says no one is more trustworthy than Marcus Steele." I cocked my head. "I say the only person more trustworthy is you."

He was silent, just staring at me.

I held up the mug. He took it, turning it until he pressed his mouth over the same spot where mine had been.

My belly clenched. God, it was like flames igniting inside me.

"I've tried to stay away from you," he said.

My heart thumped. "Why?"

He set the mug down. "Because we're friends. Because I'm older than you."

"Only by a few years."

"Because we're family and grew up together."

"I don't think of you as my brother, Jameson."

"I know." His deep voice was a low rumble. "My feelings for you are not brotherly."

My chest hitched. "How do you feel?"

His gaze ran down my body. "Those fucking shorts. I can see all of those legs of yours. And I know you've got nothing on under that shirt. All of you is pure temptation."

My skin flushed. "I like you too, Jameson. Believe me, I've come on my own fingers plenty of times thinking of you."

He groaned—a low masculine sound. "I'm just a soldier, Greer. I'm not smart, I don't have any degrees, I..."

I took a step forward. "That's why you pushed me away?"

"Part of it. I'm not good enough for—"

Now I was angry. I shoved his chest. "Bullshit. Jesus, I had a smart guy—" I made air quotes when I said smart "—and he wanted me to be his baby-making machine."

Jameson growled. "He was an idiot. I'll kick his ass."

"I already did. He's just a distant memory now." I moved closer to him. "The best man I know, he's strong and loyal and trustworthy. And he sees me."

"When I look at you, I see intelligence and beauty."

"Jameson—"

He scooped me up and set me on the island. I gasped, then his mouth was on mine.

Pulling him closer, I lost myself in the kiss. I drowned in it. I savored the scrape of his stubble, the masculine taste of him, the pure heat.

"I need more." His voice was gritty, raising goosebumps on my skin. He nipped at my jaw. "I need to taste you."

Then his big hands gripped the waistband of the shorts.

My chest hitched. *Oh, god.*

Then he ripped them down my legs. He also discovered that I wasn't wearing any panties.

"Greer," he growled.

Jameson

I COULDN'T THINK. I had my hands on Greer. All I could do was feel her, smell her, hear the excited hitch in her breathing.

Fuck.

Need pounded inside me—hot, relentless. I ran my hands up her bare legs, listening to her small gasps. She wasn't wearing any panties. I parted her thighs. In the shadows of the kitchen, it was like no one else existed. It was just us.

I pushed her back flat on the counter and her lips parted. Her gaze locked on mine.

"So damn beautiful." I lowered my head and

pushed her shirt up. I peppered kisses across her stomach. Her skin was smooth, and I felt her shiver under my lips.

"God, Jameson." Her voice was husky.

Greer. I was finally touching Greer. I pushed her thighs apart even wider. If I didn't taste her, I'd lose my mind.

I ran my mouth up her inner thigh.

She made a choked sound, her hands twisting in my hair.

Then, my mouth was finally—finally!—on her sweet pussy.

So. Fucking. Good.

I licked and explored her sweetness. She made a garbled sound, tugging on my hair. I licked at her—she was slick, and her honey-musk taste filled my senses. She pushed her body closer, arching to my mouth.

"Perfect. So damn perfect." I found the swollen nub of her clit and circled it with my tongue.

"*Jameson.*"

"You have no idea," he growled. "No fucking idea how you affect me. How much I want you all the damn time."

Her lips parted. She stared at me.

I went back to eating her—licking, sucking until she was making incoherent sounds and writhing for me.

I slid my finger inside her. She was tight and slick. How would it feel to slide my cock inside her?

Savoring the sounds she made, I kept licking, feeling her nails on my skin. Then her body tensed. She was close.

I closed my lips on her clit and sucked. With a sharp cry, she came, crying out my name.

Watching her come was the best thing I'd ever seen. I rubbed my mouth against her thigh, watching the pleasure wash over her.

Damn. My gut was hot and tight. I'd made Greer come. That felt like an honor.

Her eyes opened, were slightly dazed, and we looked at each other. She cupped my face, her nails rasping on my stubble.

"More," she murmured.

Need shot straight through my cock. My fingers tightened on her legs. "How much more?"

She licked her lips. "Everything."

I was just about to haul her closer and take her to her quarters when my communicator pinged.

I cursed and dropped my chin to my chest. Talk about colossal bad timing. I didn't want to answer it. It pinged again.

"Answer it, Jameson," she murmured.

Biting back a curse, I yanked it off my belt. "Steele."

"Jameson." Kai's voice. "We have movement in the trees to the east."

I closed my eyes. Sometimes being the one in charge, being responsible, sucked. "On my way."

There was a beat of silence.

"You need to go." Greer sat up.

"Yeah, but I don't want to."

She gave me a small smile, a real one. I was damn glad to see it.

"I really don't want you to go either." She leaned forward.

The kiss was quick but deep, and I knew she tasted herself on my lips.

"I'll see you in the morning," she murmured.

I nodded.

"And thanks."

"You never have to thank me for making you come."

She slid off the counter and pulled her pajama shorts back on. "As long as you do it again."

I could only manage a nod. My communicator pinged again and I muttered a curse.

"Go." She pulled a face. "I need to clean up in here."

I reached out and ran my finger down her bare shoulder, then I turned and forced myself to walk out.

"Jameson?"

I looked back.

"Be careful."

I nodded, then strode down the corridor.

You have a damn job to do, Steele.

But all I could think about was Greer.

CHAPTER NINE

Jameson

The cow gave a low, indignant moo.

Marc tugged on the rope. "Come on, Bessie."

"You named it?" Zeke said incredulously.

"I didn't want to just call her cow."

"We're using it to lure a monster. It could get eaten."

Marc covered Bessie's ears. "Hey, don't tell her that, bro."

I sighed. "Get the cow up on the dam wall." I spotted Maxim coming out of the workshop holding the spherical electro device. His dark hair was tied back in a short tail at the base of his neck. "We need to be ready to deploy the electro weapon, but we need a monster first."

The twins nodded and the cow mooed.

It was a bright, crisp morning. Even though the sun was hot on my skin, the temperature was nice.

A perfect day for monster hunting.

I strode over to meet Maxim. "All ready?"

He nodded. "It's ready. Like I said, the best impact will be if the monster swallows the device. If it just goes off in the water beside the monster, I can't guarantee the result. "

"Yeah, we have a plan for that."

Maxim looked at the cow and lifted a brow.

"Whatever gets the job done," I said. "I prefer it eating a cow than one of us." I turned to the water, letting my gaze run over the lake. The water was still. No sign of the monster this morning.

The base door opened, and Greer strode out.

Instantly, I felt lighter. Memories of last night filled my head.

She spotted me and smiled. "Good morning."

"Morning. Sleep well?"

"Extremely well." She shot me a private smile. Then she turned to look at the device in Maxim's hands. "It's ready? I thought it would be bigger."

"It's big enough to get the job done," Maxim said. "But it needs to be inside the monster."

Greer frowned. "What? Did you say *inside*?"

"Jameson has a plan."

She whirled. "You're going to put that *inside* the creature that's already killed two people?" The cow mooed. Greer's eyes widened. "Oh God."

"You keep your people back." I could see several of the engineers hovering by the door.

"Can I have a word? In private." She grabbed my sleeve and dragged me around the corner of the base entrance and out of view of the others. "This is dangerous."

There was worry in her voice.

"My work is dangerous, Greer." I cupped her cheek. "But the guys and I know what we're doing. We're good at this."

"I don't want you to get hurt."

"That's not on my agenda for today." I lowered my head and nibbled at her lips.

She clung to me. With a groan, I deepened the kiss. She kissed me back enthusiastically

I had to force myself to set her down. I squeezed her hip. "I've got to get back to the squad."

"Be careful out there, Jameson." She grabbed my shirt. "I promise you all kinds of sexual favors if you come back to me in one piece."

I instantly went hard. "All kinds?"

"Yes." She released me. "Now, go do your thing."

I couldn't resist another quick, hard kiss. "I'll be back. And Greer, I'll be looking to cash in on that promise." I strode back out onto the dam wall, energized. "All right, Hunter Squad, let's do this."

Maxim pressed some buttons on the electro device and a hum came from the weapon. "It's armed and ready."

He handed it over and my hands closed on the cool metal. I felt a low pulse coming from it.

"I have the control." Maxim held up a small remote control. "I'll stand up here on the dam wall and when it's in position, I'll activate it."

Zeke and Marc had the cow by the edge of the water. Kai and North stood nearby with carbines in hand, watching for the monster.

I walked to the cow, then I glanced back. Greer and her team were high on the wall. She nodded.

"Let's ring the dinner bell," I said.

The Talon appeared overhead, the wash from its rotors catching my hair. Colbie flew out over the water.

"Releasing cargo," she said across the comm line.

Cow blood tipped from the cargo hold and hit the water. Then the Talon flew back toward the dam wall, leaving a trail that led right to Bessie.

"I have movement in the water," Sasha said on comms.

"It's coming," Kai murmured.

There were ripples far out in the water. The monster was arrowing right toward the chum. It moved through the trail of blood like a heat-seeking missile.

"Look sharp." My hands tightened on the electro weapon. I reached over and tied the device to the cow's collar.

The monster reared out of the water.

Fuck me. It looked bigger than it had seemed yesterday. Six tentacles were waving, and that huge sucker mouth in the center of the black, oily body came into view.

Bessie went crazy, snapping the rope.

Shit. I grabbed for her, but she rammed into me. I managed to rip the electro device off her, just before she ran off along the dam wall.

Okay. Plan B.

Clutching the weapon tightly, I zeroed in on the monster's sucker mouth and pulled my arm back. I tossed the device.

It sailed toward the creature's mouth.

Yes. Come on.

A tentacle whipped through the air. It hit the device, and I watched as the electro weapon hit the water with a splash. It bobbed there like a beach ball.

My gut clenched. *No, dammit.*

The tentacle changed direction and sailed right at me. I dropped to the ground, and it swung past my head. I heard Kai and the others open fire.

I looked up, and saw the tentacle reaching farther than it ever had before. Jeez, how long was it?

Then my chest locked. It was aiming right at Greer and the other engineers.

I leaped to my feet. "Watch out!"

The engineers all scrambled. The tentacle curled around Lisa, and I heard Greer shouting. She kicked at the tentacle.

Then Lisa was yanked off the wall and into the air. Her screams were piercing.

The tentacle pulled her into the water with a splash.

Hell. I ran. I didn't stop to think. I dropped my carbine and then I dove off the wall and into the water.

Greer

NO.

My heart was beating so hard it hurt.

The monster had taken Lisa.

And Jameson had just dove in after her.

Oh, my God.

I raced down the stairs. Kai, North, Zeke, and Marc were all firing on the creature. The tentacle came up, Lisa still wrapped in it and soaking wet. She was screaming.

The monster screeched.

Where was Jameson?

I searched the water frantically. I couldn't lose him. I'd just finally gotten him to see me.

I had feelings for him and I knew there was the possibility of so much more. He was *mine*. I knew it. Hell, somewhere inside me, I'd known it for a long time.

The monster screeched so loudly I stopped and clapped my hands over my ears.

"There he is," Kai yelled.

I lowered my hands and saw Jameson pulling himself up on a tentacle. He started stabbing at it with his knife. It was the tentacle holding Lisa.

He sawed his blade into the flesh. I saw black, sludge-like blood dripping into the water.

The tentacle waved violently, and Lisa went flying. She hit the water with a splash.

"I've got her." Kai shoved his carbine at me. "Greer, keep firing."

I nodded.

As Kai dove into the water, all my worry for Lisa and Jameson solidified. I raced to the edge of the dam wall and lifted the weapon. My father was a sniper, and I'd been shooting since I was a little girl. A gun felt all too familiar in my hands. I was my father's daughter, after all.

I saw Jameson leap off the tentacle. He started cutting through the water, heading back to the wall.

The monster was thrashing. Black blood filled the water, floating like an oil slick. Then the creature turned and its gaze locked on Jameson.

It started swimming toward him, accelerating quickly.

No.

I aimed and fired.

North appeared beside me, concentrating his fire in the same location as mine.

"Jameson, swim faster," North said into his earpiece.

God, the monster was gaining on him. I switched, aiming for one of the creature's red eyes.

Direct hit.

The monster stopped, thrashing wildly.

"North, aim for the eyes."

"Got it." He adjusted his aim. "Shit, that's a small target. How the hell did you hit it?"

We kept firing, but the creature lifted its tentacles, blocking our laser fire. It resumed chasing after Jameson, its mouth gaping open. It lunged, sending a large wave of water toward us.

Jameson disappeared under the water.

Under the damn monster.

"Jameson!" I screamed.

Water splashed up onto the dam wall and North yanked me back.

There was a wash of air. The Talon flew into view, hovering over the dam wall. There were two ropes dangling beneath it.

Then, two powerful bodies were running along the dam wall—Zeke and Marc.

Both men leaped up and grabbed the ropes.

My heart leaped into my throat. They held on as the quadcopter moved over the water.

Over the monster.

The twins were firing directly down onto it. The creature let out more ear-splitting shrieks, and the water churned. I lifted my carbine and kept firing.

The Talon dodged two waving tentacles. It was a hell of a display of Colbie's flying skills.

Come on, Jameson. I scanned the water. *Where was he?*

I refused to believe that he was gone. Refused to believe that he was inside that horrible creature.

Suddenly, I saw his head break the water. He powered toward the dam wall.

The relief was so strong it almost drove me to my knees.

He was pulling something behind him. I gasped. He'd found the electro weapon.

I refocused on the monster, firing until my carbine ran out of charge. Dangling below the Talon, I saw Zeke dropping something onto the monster.

Boom. Boom. Boom.

The grenades detonated.

With a squeal, the monster sank into the water and swam away. It disappeared from view, leaving only a ripple in the water.

I sagged. *God.* Adrenaline charged inside me.

"Everyone okay?" North touched a finger to his ear. "Good."

I spotted Kai with a sodden Lisa. He was helping her up the ladder and onto the dam wall.

I ran down toward them. "Lisa, are you all right?" Her braid had come loose and her hair stuck to her cheeks.

"No." The woman's voice was shaky. "Hell the fuck no."

"I've got her." North wrapped an arm around the woman. "I'll take you down to the infirmary."

"I want sedatives. The good stuff. Don't hold out on me."

I fought back a smile. She was going to be okay.

Kai stood and shook the water off.

A moment later, Jameson appeared at the ladder. "Kai." He handed the electro weapon up to the other man.

I stared at Jameson, a million emotions storming around inside me. He'd almost died.

He reached the top and straightened, running a hand over his head and shaking off some water.

"Are you all right?" My voice was tight.

"Yeah."

I strode up to him. "Are you *insane*?" I smacked his chest. "You dove into the water with a giant monster."

"I had to save Lisa. And we needed to get the electro weapon."

"You risked your life. You almost got eaten." I realized my voice had risen several notches.

"Hey." He grabbed my hands, holding them to his chest. "It's okay, Greer. I'm okay."

I wasn't. I couldn't get a hold on my emotions.

All I could think about was losing him.

"Take a deep breath," he said.

I managed to drag one in, then another. That's when I saw a deep scratch on his neck and shoulder. It was smeared with black, oily, monster blood.

"You're hurt, and you've got monster goop on you. It could be poisonous."

"North will—"

"No, he's busy with Lisa. I'll look at you."

Jameson eyed me. "All right." He looked at the people hovering nearby. "Everyone, that's it for now. Let's regroup."

I took his hand and tugged him toward the base door.

CHAPTER TEN

Jameson

I let Greer pull me into her quarters. Tension was vibrating off her.

She'd been scared.

For me.

My dad had scared my mom plenty of times. He'd told me that he let her process it by staying silent, and giving her whatever she needed.

Greer pressed the door control and it slid closed.

"Take your armor and clothes off," she said.

"Ah…"

She reached up and started unfastening my chest armor. "No arguments. Get in the shower, Jameson. We need to get this muck off you."

"Okay." I stripped off my armor and set it against the wall. In the bathroom, I shed my wet clothes and stepped under the spray.

Then I turned and a jolt ran through me.

Greer stood in the doorway watching me.

Through the steamy glass she unashamedly looked at my body. My cock hardened, lengthened, and I saw her chest hitch.

She shot me a look, then walked back into the bedroom.

I quickly soaped up, then did it again. I knew better than to leave any monster crud on my body. Finally, I shut the water off, and toweled myself dry.

I looked at my reflection in the mirror. Yeah, maybe I wasn't a head-turner, and my body had more than a few scars. But Greer wanted me.

And I wanted her. Damn any consequences.

I wrapped the towel around my waist and stepped out of the bathroom.

Greer was standing by a chair. There was a first aid kit open on the table.

"Sit." She pointed at the chair.

I sat and saw her gaze run over my bare chest. I cleared my throat. "I already have a few scars. Another one isn't a problem."

She lifted her hand and traced a scar on my pec. It was an old one I'd gotten from monster claws. It had happened when I'd been young and cocky and new to the squad. I'd learned to move faster after that.

Then her fingers moved up to the raw marks on my neck, and my thoughts scattered.

"This one *isn't* going to scar." She reached into the first aid kit, then started cleaning the wound.

I controlled my wince at the sting and at the tart anger in her voice.

"I did my job, Greer. Sometimes, I have to take risks to save lives."

"You were almost killed."

"No, I trust my squad. I knew they'd have my back." I touched her chin and our gazes met. "And I knew you'd have my back. I saw you with the carbine. You're a hell of a shot. Used to drive me crazy when we were kids that you were better than me with a carbine. I always wanted to impress you."

"You did. You do." She sighed. "You're so damn brave, a damn hero. You saved Lisa's life."

"I'm sorry you were scared."

"I don't want to lose you."

I grabbed her hand. "Not gonna happen."

She nodded. "Now, hold still." She applied some med gel to my scratch. I felt a tingle as it worked. Then she pressed a bandage over the deepest part of the angry gash.

I absorbed the brush of her fingers. Her hands were on me, and I liked that so damn much. I was already fighting a hard-on, and the towel didn't hide very much.

"I'm going to give you a shot to fight off any infection." She pressed a pressure injector to the side of my neck.

"Thanks, Greer."

"I'm not done yet."

I looked up. Then I watched as she set the injector back into the first aid kit, then sank to her knees in front of me. She pressed her hands to my thighs.

My muscles tensed. "Greer?"

"Your injuries are treated, but... I need more."

I cocked my head, my abs tight.

"I need to know that you're okay, that you're alive." Her slim hands moved up—over my abs, to my chest. I sucked in a breath. The touch was electric. Her fingers traced over my muscles, downward, and over the ridges of my abs.

"I love your body," she murmured.

"I like yours better." My throat was tight.

Then she pushed the towel open.

Fuck.

My rock-hard cock sprang free, standing up at attention. Her lips parted, and I saw the need on her face.

"Greer... I'm yours. Whatever you want."

"I want you, Jameson. So much." She wrapped a hand around my cock. "I want you in my mouth."

Shit. This was happening. Greer was touching me. Greer's hand was squeezing my cock. Greer was going to suck me.

Everything inside me throbbed and I reached out, spearing a hand into her hair. "Whatever you want, beautiful, I'll give it to you."

Her breathing was fast as she looked at me. All I saw was the desire filling her eyes.

She leaned forward and licked the head of my cock.

It ripped a groan from me. My fingers tightened in her hair, and she whimpered. Then, she wrapped her lips around my cock and sucked me deep.

I gritted my teeth, watching as she took her time, her head bobbing on my cock, going a little deeper each time.

The sight of her...

Shit. I fought off my impending climax. I didn't want this to be over too soon.

She sucked harder, and I hissed. "Shit, Greer. Yes, just like that."

She kept sucking, and seeing my cock buried deep in her tempting mouth, tipped me closer to the edge. My head dropped back and all I could do was feel.

"Greer, your mouth… It's so good."

I looked back at her, at the way her lips were stretched around me, the way her cheeks hollowed as she sucked.

I wasn't going to last much longer.

"Jesus, beautiful—" My hips bumped up and she gagged briefly, but didn't pull off. Her hands clenched on my thighs, and she took me deeper.

"I'm coming, Greer." My voice sounded like gravel.

As she sucked me, I tugged on her hair. I groaned out a curse, then I was coming, shooting my hot load into her mouth. Greer drank down every drop.

Greer

I SAT BACK, but could barely stay still. Desire was humming through me. I rocked on my knees. I felt empty, achy. My heart was racing and I could still taste Jameson on my tongue.

His groans, the way it had felt to pleasure him… I loved the way I'd driven him over the edge. My belly throbbed, way down low.

A big hand cupped my face and his eyes were filled with warmth.

"You beautiful thing. You have no idea what you do to me."

I shifted again. I ached so much.

His gaze sharpened. "Are you turned on, Greer?"

I nodded.

"Hungry?"

"For you."

He slid his hands under my armpits and hauled me up. I loved his strength. I straddled him and his skin was hot against mine.

"I don't deserve you," he said.

"That's crap. I'm offering myself because I want you so much." Memories of what had happened earlier tried to intrude. I'd almost lost him.

"Hey, stay here with me," he said.

I nodded, then I leaned forward and pressed my mouth to his. With a groan, he took full control. His tongue thrust into my mouth, and I kissed him back. I wanted him with an urgency that should have scared me.

Soon I was panting from the kiss.

"I want to be deep inside you." His voice was a low growl that shivered through me. "I've wanted that for a long time."

"Me too. I'm all yours."

"Good." His hands squeezed my hips. "Show me. Take your clothes off."

"Is that an order?" I asked breathily.

His hazel eyes glittered. "Yes."

I slid off him. I took my clothes off fast, until I was

only wearing black panties. His hot gaze was on me, taking its time to catalogue my almost-naked body. There was no doubt how much he liked to look at me.

I looked back. At his chest, then lower. His cock was hard again, and I sucked in a breath.

Then I gripped his shoulders for balance and climbed back on. Only a thin layer of lace separated me from that thick cock.

Jameson muttered a curse, his muscles tense and hard. He made me feel powerful. I loved seeing how much I affected him.

"You have a contraceptive implant?" he asked.

I nodded. The small implant protected against pregnancy and disease. I rocked against him and slid a hand down my belly. "Do you know how much I ache for you?"

"Show me."

I slid my fingers into the lace, touching my sensitive clit. I gasped.

His hands ran along my sides and he pulled me closer. Then he sucked one of my nipples into his hot mouth.

"*Oh.*" Sensations rocketed through me. I arched my back, knowing he'd hold me.

"Fuck, the things I want to do to you."

"So do them. I'm yours. My body is yours, Jameson."

"What I want is my cock lodged deep in this slick, needy pussy." His hand joined mine in my panties, stroking me.

I let out a moan. I was already so wet, but he had a big cock, and I knew I'd feel it.

He gripped the side of my panties and yanked. I heard the lace tear, and a thrill of desire throbbed through me. I reached down and circled his cock. He let out a throaty groan.

I positioned him between my thighs, the fat head nestling between my folds.

"*Fuck.*" His hands clenched on my ass.

"I'm going to feel every inch of this." I sank down. I took him, inch by thick inch, inside me. "Jameson, you're so big." The last word turned to a moan. I felt my inner muscles stretching. And I saw the muscles in his neck and arms straining.

"Baby, you feel so good."

My ass touched his muscular thighs. He was as deep as he could go. I lifted up and dropped back down. A moan ripped from me.

"You're so damn tight." His voice was pure grit. "Ride me, Greer."

I moved faster and found a rhythm. *Oh, God.* Electricity shot through me. I twisted my hips, moving quicker, needing more.

"*Fuck.*" He thrust up.

I cried out. His hands gripped my ass, urging me on. Working me up and down on his cock.

Then his mouth was on mine. The kiss was deep, filled with pure possession.

When our lips pulled apart, I let my mouth travel over that strong jaw, then down to his neck. I bit the tendon.

"*Yes,*" he growled. "I knew you'd be the one. The best I've ever had."

My belly contracted. I was going to come soon. It was impossible to hold back.

Flesh slapped against flesh. His fingers tightened on my ass, driving me down harder. Then one big hand moved between our surging bodies. He found my swollen clit and worked it hard.

"Oh…oh." Every muscle was tight and my legs were shaking.

"Come for me, gorgeous Greer. Now. I want to hear you scream."

I threw my head back, pleasure crashing through me. "Jameson!"

My vision blurred, and I was afraid the intensity of the pleasure would make me black out.

Jameson surged up out of the chair, and I gasped. With his cock still inside me, he crossed to my bed. My back hit the covers, his big body over mine, in mine.

He thrust hard, filling me in every way.

I screamed his name. My pulse pounded as I held on. I dug my heels into his ass and gripped his biceps.

I came again. Sensation burned through me.

He thrust deep and stayed there. He let out a low roar as he came.

Afterward, all I could do was cling to him. Air sawed in and out of my lungs. My body was still twitching.

What had that been? Sex had never been so all-consuming.

He nuzzled my throat. "You okay?"

"Jameson…" My voice cracked. "That wasn't anywhere near okay. It was in a different stratosphere."

He let out a low chuckle. He pulled out of me, then lay down beside me. His hands ran over my body.

"I didn't hurt you? I was rough."

I cupped his stubbled jaw. "Apparently, I really like rough."

He gave me a lopsided smile.

"I thought I lost you today," I whispered.

His smile flattened. He slid a hand into my hair. "I'm okay, beautiful. I think I just proved that." His other hand smoothed over my shoulder, then cupped my breast. My nipple pebbled. "Maybe you need more convincing?"

My pulse went crazy. "Maybe I do." I pulled his head down to mine.

CHAPTER ELEVEN

Jameson

"Get there, Greer."

Gripping her hips, I plunged into her from behind. She let out a husky cry. Damn, I loved the sounds she made when I was fucking her.

With a moan, she gripped the vanity in her bathroom, pushing back against me.

"I want to feel you come on my cock, beautiful."

"*Jameson.*" She slid a hand between her thighs.

"That's it, touch your clit."

"Yes. I can feel where you're stretching me."

I groaned, my muscles tightening. "I'm going to come soon, but you first." I wrapped one arm under her and across her middle, holding her in place. I drove into her and then buried my face in her neck. Breathing in the scent of her, I absorbed the feeling of being joined to her.

On my next thrust, her pussy clamped down. She cried out my name and that triggered my own orgasm.

I looked up and our gazes locked in the mirror. Her lips parted and she stared back.

That connection rocked through me. She was made for me, and me for her. I pulled out of her, and gripped my cock and spurted over her ass and lower back. "Fuck, Greer. All mine."

She looked over her shoulder, flushed and smiling. "Did you just mark me?"

"Yeah." I leaned forward and kissed her, nibbling at her lips.

"I need to shower again now," she murmured. "That's not a complaint. Not after the best, hottest sex I've ever had."

Warmth filled my gut. "I'm not sorry." I pressed a kiss to her bare shoulder blade. "I'll make us breakfast while you clean up."

Back in her quarters, I pulled on a T-shirt and cargo pants. Reality would come storming back in soon. Right now, I didn't want to think about damn monsters. I wanted to enjoy these last few minutes where it was just the two of us.

I moved over to the food printer, programmed it for eggs, and stilled. This wouldn't be our last time together. We'd have hundreds of mornings together, thousands of nights, countless times where I'd slide inside her and make her cry out my name.

I was claiming Greer Baird as mine.

Rightness spread through me.

Me and Greer.

Yes, I'd have to face her parents, but there would be no messy break up because she was mine. I wanted her, not for just a few months. Forever.

I sucked in a breath. We'd never have long conversations about differential equations or thermodynamics—I shuddered at the thought—but I'd make her happy. I'd make it so she never, ever regretted being mine.

The printer dinged. The eggs were ready.

I just needed Greer to get on board with it. After we destroyed this monster.

Greer appeared, fluffing her blonde hair. She was wearing dark pants and a khaki shirt. "I'm starving."

"I'm not surprised." I pulled the plates out of the printer. "You burned lots of calories last night."

She grinned. "In the best possible way."

I kissed her, then set a plate down in front of her, along with a mug of coffee.

I'd just sat down with my own breakfast when the door chimed. I strode over and when I opened it, I found my squad mates.

"Something smells good." Marc strolled past me. "Eggs. I need some eggs." He made a beeline to the food printer.

Kai nodded, glanced at Greer, then smiled.

I glared at him.

North walked in. "I want eggs too."

Zeke followed behind, his face inscrutable. He just nodded, then moved to the coffee pot.

I sighed. Alone time was over.

We crowded around Greer's small table, but there wasn't enough room for everyone, so North and Zeke sat on the couch.

"You two look like you slept well." Marc grinned.

I threw some eggs at him.

"It's about time, is all I can say," Kai said.

"What do you mean?" Greer asked.

Marc snorted. "You've been pining for each other for ages."

I frowned. "No one's been pining." I was starting to hate that word.

"Fine," Marc said. "How about yearning, longing, craving...?"

"Do you want this coffee poured over your head?" I said.

Greer giggled, and I relaxed a little.

"Marc's right," North added. "You were both too stubborn to do anything about it."

"Don't you start," I growled. "We don't need your help."

Greer smiled at me. "No, we don't."

"So what's our plan for our monster friend?" Marc asked.

The eggs turned to dust in my mouth. I grabbed my coffee mug and drained it. "We need a new plan."

The door chimed. When Marc opened it, Colbie appeared. "No one told me there was a party. Ooh, eggs."

Maxim followed the pilot in, looking dark and brooding. His black hair was loose today, almost brushing his shoulders.

"Anybody else want to join us?" I muttered.

"So, the new plan?" Kai prompted.

I rubbed the back of my neck. "Based on yesterday, we need to attack the monster away from the dam wall."

"You need more precision—" Greer interjected "—if you want to get that device inside the monster."

Maxim nodded slowly. "We could fire it off a gun."

"A crossbow would be better," Greer said. "I have a good tactical one that my dad made."

"That's a good idea." Maxim nodded, and you could practically see his mind ticking over. "I can modify it."

"If we need to be away from the dam wall, you'll need to fire it from the Talon," Colbie said, shoveling eggs into her mouth.

I nodded. "Good idea. I'll do it."

"No, I'll do it." Greer lifted her chin. "I'm the best shot and it's my crossbow."

My gut rebelled. I didn't want her anywhere near the monster. "No."

She arched a brow. "Yes. You know it's the best idea."

"She makes sense, Jameson," Colbie said quietly.

I blew out a breath. Greer and all my squad were looking at me. Dammit. My hand clenched on my coffee mug.

"Jameson," Greer said.

"Okay," I bit out. "But I'm in charge of this mission. You listen to me."

She nodded.

I'd be right beside her. Every step of the way.

Kai sat back in his chair. "We need to lure the monster out where we want it."

"Not poor Bessie again," Marc said.

"I think our monster prefers human bait," I said.

Marc nodded. "I'll dangle from the rappel line under the Talon."

"What?" Colbie said. "That's *insane*."

Marc shrugged. "Zeke and I have dangled off the Talon loads of times before. It makes sense. Besides you're the pilot. If I get eaten, it's on you, sparrow."

"Don't call me that. Maybe I'll let the tentacle monster eat you."

"Nah, you'd miss my handsome face and wit."

Colbie rolled her eyes.

I didn't love any of this, but we needed to take the monster out.

One way or another.

"Okay. Maxim will modify the crossbow, Marc is the bait, and Greer will fire the device at the monster. The rest of us will provide support."

Maxim stood. "Greer, if I can have the crossbow, I'll get working rigging it so it will hold the electro device."

Greer hurried over to a cabinet.

"All right." I met everyone's gazes. "Hunter Squad, let's do what we do best."

"Kick some monster ass," Marc said.

And stay alive while we did it.

Greer

THE MORNING HAD PASSED in a blur of preparation. Maxim had rigged my crossbow so it would fire the electro device. I hefted it now. With the device attached to it, it was much heavier.

I'd practiced with it several times. We'd set up a

target on the grass near the dam, and Maxim had given me a dummy device that was the same weight as the electro weapon.

"You're a damn good shot," he said.

I snorted. "I'm not just an engineer, I'm Shaw Baird's daughter."

"True."

"You're the same. You didn't take after your dad on the art side, but what you do, inventing, it's kind of an art."

Maxim's father Nico was a brilliant painter. But I was well aware he'd been a lot of other things during the invasion, along with Maxim's soldier mother, Mackenna.

"I'm pretty handy with a knife, like dad." Maxim smiled.

Looking back at the target, I dragged in a breath.

I had to get this right. If I failed…

He stepped closer and pressed a hand to my shoulder. "You've got this."

"Right, all I have to do is aim at a giant monster from a moving quadcopter. A monster is a little different than that target." I nodded my head.

"Hunter Squad will be with you." He cocked a brow. "Besides, our fearless leader won't let you get hurt."

"I know."

Like I'd summoned him, Jameson appeared. He was dressed in his armor, his face grim. He looked tough. My rough, passionate lover from last night was nowhere in sight.

"Ready?" he asked.

"As I'll ever be."

"Just think, soon, the monster will be dead."

I swallowed. "I know."

Maxim nodded. "Good luck. As soon as I know the device is inside the monster, I'll detonate it with the remote. I'm going to check on the others." He strode away.

"You're worried," Jameson said after he'd left.

"Of course I'm worried. That creature almost killed you and Lisa yesterday."

He rested his hands on my shoulders.

"I don't want to lose you, Jameson. Not when I just finally have you."

He hauled me in for a hard kiss. I gripped his shoulders and kissed him back, filling the kiss with all my rioting emotions.

"I'm not going anywhere," he said. "I have armor for you to wear. I'll be with you every step of the way. Right beside you."

I nodded.

He led me over to an open crate, then helped me strap the armor on. I'd seen my parents' old armor. It used to be bulkier, and theirs was covered in scratches and dings from countless fights. I was the daughter of Claudia and Shaw Baird. I could do this, just like they had, hundreds of times.

Jameson took my hand. "Ready?"

I lifted my chin. "Let's do this."

He held out his palm. There was a small device resting on it. "Earpiece. You'll be in constant contact with me, the squad, and Sasha."

I carefully slipped it into my ear and he checked it. His fingers brushed along the shell of my ear.

We walked off the dam wall toward the Talon parked on the grass. Sunlight gleamed off the gray metal. Colbie was doing her preflight checks and waved.

Kai, North, and the twins were already in their armor. God, they were something to look at. Tough and sexy as hell.

Not quite as tough and sexy as my man.

My man. I controlled my inner jolt.

"All right." Marc smiled. "We're ready to rock and roll and kick some monster ass."

"You're about to dangle from the Talon over a killer monster," I said dryly.

He winked. "Fun, right?"

I shook my head.

"All right, Hunter Squad," Jameson said. "Let's move out."

He helped me aboard the Talon. It had a large central area, with several rows of seats. There was a large turret at the back where an operator could sit.

Colbie climbed into the cockpit at the front and pulled a helmet over her head. She started humming as she swiped the control panel and flicked switches. The engines started. The others all sat in their seats, joking around.

I tried to take some calming breaths. Jameson sat across from me and squeezed my knee.

"Hold on, everyone," Colbie called back.

The Talon lifted off and my belly swooped.

Normally, I liked to fly. I looked out the window at the trees, and smiled.

Then, the dam came into view. It looked big from up here. My gaze shifted to the forest, green and vital, and the dark water, stretching all the way south. I straightened in my seat. This project was important. People needed this water. If we wanted to grow and expand, we had to succeed in killing this monster.

We were going to do this.

"Release the bait," Colbie said.

"Funny, little sparrow." Marc checked his harness and where he was attached to the rappel cord.

Jameson slid the side door open.

"Be careful," Zeke told his brother.

Marc clasped his brother's arm. "Always."

"No, you're not," Zeke said.

"More like never," Colbie added from the cockpit.

Marc looked at me. "See what I have to put up with." He raised his voice. "Don't let me get eaten, sparrow."

"We'll see." There was a pause from the cockpit. "Be careful."

With a wave, Marc leaped out the open side door of the quadcopter.

I gasped. He had no fear.

Jameson stood at the edge of the door, gripping the doorframe. I moved up beside him, resting the crossbow on the seat nearby.

I looked out the door.

The dark-blue water looked like glass below. Marc dangled several meters below us and several meters above the water.

"Come on, Nessie," Marc yelled, loud enough that we could just hear him. "This harness chafes."

I shook my head. His carefree attitude helped calm my nerves. But mostly, it was Jameson's steady presence beside me.

"We have contact."

I jolted at Sasha's steady voice in my ear.

Everybody turned serious. I felt like electricity skated through the cabin of the Talon.

"Ten o'clock," Colbie called back.

Jameson swiveled and I followed his gaze.

I saw it. The churning ripple in the water, heading our way. My mouth went dry.

"Marc, here it comes," Jameson said.

"I see her."

"It might be male," Colbie said.

"Nah, it's definitely a she," Marc said.

I was vaguely aware of Kai, Zeke, and North on the other side of the Talon, their carbines at the ready. I grabbed the crossbow and checked the electro weapon. It was ready. I lay on the floor of the Talon, my head and shoulders poking out of the open door. Jameson crouched beside me, looking ready to grab me if needed.

Below, the monster lunged out of the water, tentacles waving. I gasped, my heart lodging in my throat. Marc swung on his line and fired down at it. The monster screeched. Its mouth was just visible above the surface.

"I need it out of the water more," I said, aiming the crossbow.

"Take him lower," Jameson ordered.

Marc's line lengthened. A tentacle swung at him, and he spun away, dodging it. Then, the creature breached the surface, reaching for our bait, its mouth open wide.

I took aim, breathed steadily.

I fired.

CHAPTER TWELVE

Jameson

I watched the electro device shoot through the air...
Straight into the monster's gaping mouth.

"The device is in place, Sasha," I yelled over the comms. "Tell Maxim. Colbie, retract the cable. Now!"

Marc started whizzing upward. I reached out and yanked Greer up.

"Nothing's happening," she cried. "It didn't work."

I kept my gaze on the monster. It reared up, trying to reach Marc. "Give Maxim time to activate it."

A second later, a low, almost subsonic sound vibrated through all of us. The monster started jerking in the water, thrashing around.

"It's working." I smiled at her. "You did it."

She beamed back at me.

The monster screeched so loudly I almost winced. I hugged Greer close, watching as the creature sagged and floated in the water.

JAMESON

It was still. Dead.

"Woo-hoo!" Marc yelled from below the Talon. He pumped a fist into the air.

I grinned back, then I turned to the rest of the squad. "It's dead."

Everyone cheered.

"Nice work, Greer," North said. "Your parents are going to be proud as hell."

She grinned, and she'd never looked more beautiful. "I'm a damn good shot. I'm going to tell Dad I'm better than him."

Then I snatched her into my arms and kissed her. She clutched at my shoulders, kissing me back.

The guys cheered again, and Kai whistled.

"Shut up," I muttered at them, but I was still smiling.

"That's justice for Travis and Sam," she whispered.

"Yeah."

"Wait—" Colbie's voice cut through the moment.

Her tense tone made me stiffen. "What's wrong?"

"There's something else coming. Sasha, are you picking anything up?" The Talon turned in midair. "There's something else in the water."

"I'm picking up a faint signature," Sasha said on the comm line. "I can't tell what it is."

I turned back to the side door and scanned the water.

"Oh no," Greer said.

There. In the distance, the water was rippling hard. Something was definitely coming.

"Hunter Squad," I said.

"We're ready," Kai said.

"Marc?"

"Yeah, more fun to come," the man answered.

"Hold us steady, Colbie." I met Greer's gaze. "Stay back."

She stepped back and gripped one of the seats.

Suddenly, a massive monster, far larger than the first one we'd just killed, reared up out of the water. Multiple tentacles broke the surface, waving wildly.

"Fuck me," Marc yelled, opening fire.

The rest of the squad fired their carbines. I jerked my weapon up and pressed the trigger.

The creature let out a low rumbling sound. Like we were just pissing it off.

"Kai, turret," I barked.

A flash of movement out of the corner of my eye as Kai jumped into the turret seat. The large gun swiveled and aimed.

Heavy laser fire hit the creature. It shuddered and let out a loud roar.

More tentacles speared upward, heading for the Talon. The quadcopter jerked quickly to the side.

I stumbled, gripping the door frame hard. I swallowed a curse.

Greer stumbled into one of the seats.

"Keep firing," I yelled.

There was no time to worry about water contamination now. Another tentacle flew up, narrowly missing Marc.

"Get Marc aboard, Colbie," I said.

But before the pilot could retract the cable, another tentacle splashed out of the water. *How many did this thing have?*

Greer staggered to my side and looked out. "Oh, God," she breathed in horror.

The tentacle circled Marc. I saw him drop his carbine and kick his legs. The tentacle tightened its grip on him, then the monster pulled.

The entire Talon dipped down toward the water. The guys started cursing. I wrapped one arm around Greer and gripped the doorframe even harder to keep my balance.

The engines droned.

"Full power, Colbie," I yelled.

The Talon straightened and the monster rose out of the water.

Then we were pulled down again, tipping to the side.

We were caught in a deadly game of tug-of-war, and Marc was trapped in the middle. I saw that he was stabbing at the tentacle. But it wasn't letting him go.

"Marc, hold on."

"Not...giving up...yet."

Dammit, he sounded in a lot of pain. The damn creature was crushing him.

"Colbie, tell me you can get us free," I barked.

"That's everything I've got," she yelled back.

My mind whirled. I needed options.

"Jameson," Marc's strained voice in my earpiece. "Cut the cable."

"No!" I heard Zeke roar behind me.

My chest solidified, felt like fucking concrete. I could cut the cable. My gaze locked on Marc below us. My gut clenched. Greer's hand pressed over mine.

No. We never fucking left a man or woman behind.

"We're *not* cutting the cable. We leave *no one* behind. Okay—" I pulled out my combat knife "—let's—"

Greer broke away and reached behind us. Then she stepped into the open door beside me, the crossbow in her hands.

"Let's make this fucking monster regret its actions." She aimed the crossbow, then fired several bolts down at the monster.

The creature let out a muted roar and loosened its hold on Marc a little.

"Concentrate fire on its head," she said.

Everyone aimed their carbines at the creature's head. The monster jerked, shaking its massive bulk.

"That's it," I yelled. "Keep firing."

Then, a second tentacle speared up, and grabbed the body of the Talon.

Fuck.

Black, oily skin dotted with suckers was right in front of me. The guys were shouting, Colbie was yelling, and the Talon tilted.

Greer slipped, and the crossbow fell from her hands, dropping into the water below. We listed even more to the side. She slid toward the open door.

"Greer!"

She fell but grabbed the bottom of the doorway, her body dangling out of the quadcopter. Her gaze met mine.

I could see her fingers slipping.

"Greer! No!" I lunged for her.

Then she fell.

I watched her arms and legs flailing as she fell past a tentacle and hit the water.

No.

For a second, I couldn't breathe, couldn't think. Then my focus solidified. I had to save my squad, and I sure as hell had to save my woman.

I leaped out of the Talon and onto one of the tentacles.

Clamping my arms and legs onto it, I slid a little. I clamped on harder. Then I pulled out my knife and stabbed it deep, and the tentacle jerked.

I used all my weight and dragged the knife through the thick skin. I heard that roar-shriek again.

The creature released the Talon. I clung to the tentacle like I was riding a bucking bull. It waved through the air, whipping me around. I stabbed again.

Then it released Marc.

"Colbie, get out of range. Now!"

I watched the quadcopter turn and ascend, Marc swinging below it. He was limp in the harness, his arm and legs dangling. Shit, I hoped to hell he was all right.

The tentacle sliced sideways, and I hung on with everything I had. My body slipped a little and I gritted my teeth.

I looked down. Greer was in the water and swimming away, trying to get to the bank. But as I watched, one of the tentacles wrapped around her middle. Every muscle in my body locked.

Fucking hell. No.

I let go and plummeted into the water.

The water closed over my head, then I kicked up. I broke the surface and powered toward her.

"Greer!"

When I reached the tentacle holding her, I grabbed on.

Just then, the monster started to move, swimming through the lake and away from the Talon.

Greer

FIGHTING BACK MY PANIC, I tried to keep my head above the water. Water splashed in my eyes and filled my mouth. I spat it out.

The black tentacle tightened around me, squeezing hard.

Oh God. Oh God. There was a second monster. I couldn't believe it.

Water splashed in my face again, and I shook my head.

The monster was moving fast, swimming through the lake in the opposite direction of the dam. I was in trouble.

"Greer!"

Jameson? I heard him shout my name and wondered if I was imagining things. I turned my head.

My heart surged. He was clinging to the tentacle, just a few meters away.

He'd dove in after me. Emotion flooded me. He'd come for me.

More water splashed over us. Jameson slipped and my pulse spiked. He lunged forward, gripping on hard.

"Jameson!" I reached out, and his fingers touched mine.

Then the monster picked up speed, driving through the water.

I heard Jameson curse. I glanced up and saw the Talon above, but as the monster followed a curve in the lake, the quadcopter disappeared from view.

"I'll get you free. Hold on."

But I could tell he was struggling to hold onto the tentacle.

If he couldn't do it…

I'd be alone with the monster.

No, I wasn't going to lose it. I was going to survive this. My own mother had survived Gizzida captivity. I could survive this.

Besides all of that, I very much wanted to get naked with Jameson Steele again.

I was *very* motivated to survive.

A large wave of water hit my face. I coughed and blinked.

Then suddenly, the creature plunged *under* the water.

Darkness closed around me. I struggled wildly. I couldn't see Jameson. I couldn't see anything.

Scratching at the tentacle, I tried to loosen its grip, but it was too tight. It was impossible to break free.

I was going to drown.

I held on as long as I could, until my lungs were burning. Bubbles escaped from my mouth.

Then the creature shot upward. My head broke the surface.

I greedily sucked in air.

"Greer! Greer, are you all right?"

I blinked, my vision blurry. He was just a dark outline. "I'm...okay."

"The armor has a combat helmet built in. It has an oxygen supply. You need to activate it. There's a button on—"

The creature went under the water again.

No.

I pushed and shoved. The tentacle loosened its grip a little, then retightened. God, it hurt. What had Jameson been saying? A helmet?

Then the monster thrashed around, and water filled my mouth.

We broke the surface again and I coughed hard. "*Jameson.*"

"I'm here!"

"If I don't make it... Tell Mom and Dad I love them."

"You're going to make it." His tone was fierce, and I wished I could see him. "Activate your helmet, Greer. The button on the left side of your neck."

Helmet? I reached around, trying to find the controls. Jameson's hand appeared, as he tried to haul himself farther along the tentacle.

I touched a button, and the thin, thermoplastic helmet slid over my face. I heard a hiss of air.

He nodded, relief on his rugged face. "We're going to get out of this."

I wanted to believe him. That we were going to make it. I sucked in some deep breaths. "I want more time with you."

"And you'll get it. When this mission is over, we're going to take a few days off."

"We are? I seem to recall your mother complaining that you never take time off."

"I have a good reason to now." His voice was gruff. "We're going to spend the entire time in my bed. I'll fuck you every way I've ever dreamed of."

My heart stuttered. "You've had lots of dreams?"

"Of you? Yes."

I saw him climbing along the tentacle. He had his arms and legs clamped onto it. His helmet was in place.

My breathing hitched. I was terrified he'd fall off. "Don't leave me."

"*Never.*" His gaze stayed on mine. "Whatever happens, I'm getting you out of here."

I nodded, my breath fogging up the helmet.

"Greer, repeat that. Jameson is going to get me out of here."

"Jameson is going to get me out of here."

"Good girl. Okay, I'm—"

The monster lunged under the water again.

Oh, God. I tried to keep my breathing calm, listening to air hissing through the helmet. I pushed against the spongy, oily skin, trying to get it to loosen its hold.

Come on.

Then it shifted, and another tentacle reared into view. The end of a tentacle smacked into my face. The helmet cracked.

No. No. I stared at the spiderweb of cracks. My heart beat harder, thumping in my chest.

A thin trickle of water started pouring into the helmet. I clamped my mouth shut. The cracks widened.

It wasn't long before the facemask filled. I couldn't

hold my breath forever. Panic hit and I tried desperately to fight it back.

I couldn't hold my breath any longer.

My lips opened and water filled my mouth. I started thrashing. Black splotches filled my vision. I couldn't breathe.

My movements slowed.

Jameson.

I wasn't sure if I saw his face, or just imagined it, but then darkness bled in over everything and there was nothing.

CHAPTER THIRTEEN

HUNTER SQUAD

Jameson

The monster rocketed to the surface.

Fuck. Now I knew what a chew toy felt like. Air hissed out of the breather on my helmet. I held on tight to the spongy tentacle.

Greer. Where was Greer?

I looked up and saw her slumped in the tentacle's hold. She wasn't moving.

"Greer!" I slid along the tentacle. One wrong move and I'd lose my grip. "*Greer.*"

No response. Dammit, was she breathing?

My chest squeezed. *Hold on, baby.*

The monster was starting to slow. So far, it had ignored us. *What the hell did it want?*

The bank lay ahead of us, with a flat, grassy area. I kept crawling along the tentacle, and finally touched Greer's arm. Her skin was so cold.

"Greer?"

I lifted her head, and that's when I saw that her helmet was shattered. Her face was pale and her chest wasn't moving. Panic surged.

"Greer, baby, *no*."

The monster heaved its bulk onto the bank. I lost my grip on the slimy tentacle and slid to the ground. I hit hard on my side and rolled. I retracted my combat helmet and fought back all the aches in my body.

The tentacle released Greer, and she fell to the ground beside me.

I crawled over to her. The monster was still ignoring us, sunning itself.

"Greer." I rolled her onto her back. She wasn't breathing. I retracted what was left of her helmet.

I couldn't lose her.

I pushed her wet hair off her face, then checked her pulse and airway. "I'm not losing you, dammit. You're a fighter, Greer Baird, just like your parents."

I put my palms to her chest and started compressions. I breathed into her mouth.

"Come on." I pumped her chest. "You're mine, Greer. I plan to love you, spoil you, and annoy you for a really long time." My voice cracked. "Please don't leave me."

Emotions boiled inside my chest. I breathed into her mouth. This woman was the one that I would love for the rest of my days. I didn't want to do it without her.

She was still, her skin cold.

"Be mine. Make a life with me. Have my babies, because I want them to be smart and beautiful like you. I would never make you give up your job. The world needs your skills." My voice lowered. "I need you."

Suddenly, her body jerked. She sat up with a hacking cough.

"There you go." Relief like I'd never known rocked into me. I helped her to the side as she coughed up a bunch of water. My hand was shaking as I rubbed her back. "I've got you."

"Jameson—" her voice was hoarse. Her gaze met mine. "You didn't leave me."

"Never. I'll never leave you."

She leaned against me, and I hugged her tight.

"Thank you," she whispered.

I realized that it wasn't only my hand shaking. My entire body was shaking. "Thank you for not leaving me."

"You saved me." She pressed her face to my neck.

I touched the small pack on my belt and pulled off a tiny bottle of water. She took it from me and gulped some down, then spat the dam water taste out of her mouth.

Reaching up, I touched my earpiece. As I did, water oozed from it. *Shit*. They were built tough, but they weren't indestructible.

"Sasha, are you there?"

No response.

"Sasha? Colbie? Kai? Is anyone picking this up?"

Silence.

My jaw worked.

"They can't hear you?" Greer asked.

I shook my head. "Either the earpiece is too waterlogged or they're out of range." I saw her shift and then grimace. "Are you hurt?"

"Just sore." She lifted the bottom of her shirt up, at the bottom of her chest armor.

I saw the mottled bruises on her skin. "Damn." My fingers brushed over them gently.

"That tentacle squeezed me pretty hard, but they're just bruises." Then she stiffened, her voice lowering. "Jameson, the monster is right *there*." She looked over my shoulder.

"I know."

"God, what do we do?" she whispered.

"I'm going to kill it."

Her blue eyes went wide. "What? Alone?"

"It nearly killed you." Determination filled me. That thing had almost taken Greer from me. I grabbed her hand and pulled her up. We slowly crept behind a tree.

"Stay here."

"Jameson…"

"I've got this." I pulled some thermo grenades off my belt. "Trust me. This is what I'm good at."

She nodded, then gave me a tight hug and a quick kiss. "You're not allowed to get hurt. You promised some days off and lots of sex."

My lips curved. "I did, didn't I?"

"Be careful."

With a nod, I turned to face the creature. Its tentacles were all tucked in on itself.

It wasn't expecting us to be a risk.

I weighed the grenades carefully in my hand. My jaw tightened. This creature wouldn't kill anyone else. With the grenades in one palm, I pulled my combat knife out with the other hand.

Then I crept in closer to the monster, careful not to make a sound and disturb it.

I lifted the knife, then stabbed the closest tentacle.

It sprang awake with a low roar.

Its tentacles unfurled, waving in the air. It shifted its bulk, and a tentacle slapped down beside me. I jumped over it and stabbed again.

It made another angry sound. The tentacles whipped sideways, right at me. I dove to the ground and rolled under it.

"Come on." I looked back over my shoulder. "You've got to do better than that."

It made an awful moaning sound. Two tentacles rushed at me, and I dodged one but the second one slammed into my knees.

It knocked my legs out from under me and I fell forward. I kept the grenades tucked to my chest, rolling across the grass. Springing up, I sprinted toward the monster, leaped into the air, then stabbed my knife deep.

Another tentacle snapped out and curled around me. It lifted me off the ground.

I smiled.

Exactly as I'd hoped.

It moved me down, toward its open sucker mouth.

A nasty rotten smell hit me, and a deep sound echoed out of it. I pressed the buttons on the grenades and dropped them. One by one, they disappeared into the monster's mouth.

One. Two. Three.

There was a muffled *thump*.

The monster jerked and shrieked. Its tentacles opened and I fell.

Shit, that was a long way down.

I hit the ground hard and rolled onto my stomach. I blew out a breath, pushed through the aches, and got to my feet.

There was another larger *thump* and the monster flew apart.

As bits of oily, black skin flew around me, I ran toward the trees and dove. One more to go.

Thump.

A piece of tentacle flew past me and hit the ground. Gore sprayed dozens of feet in every direction.

I rose and looked back, grinning. The monster was in bits, black blood soaking the grass.

And I'd managed not to contaminate Greer's lake.

"Greer, it's dead."

I turned toward her. The first thing I wanted to do was kiss her.

Then I froze, every muscle in my body locking.

Two scaly humanoid monsters held Greer between them. There was something lizard-like about them. Her gaze was on mine. I could tell she was scared, but her chin was up, and her mouth was set in a flat line.

One of the monsters grunted, and a canine creature skulked forward out of the trees. It likely had dingo DNA. It had shaggy, matted fur, enormous claws on its feet, and long fangs. It growled.

JAMESON

Greer

WELL, this sucked.

I'd survived drowning, and a giant, scary, aquatic monster. Not just one, but two of them. Now I was tied up with my back pressed to Jameson's.

The two monsters who'd caught me walked upright, but were definitely not human. They had legs like tree trunks, and thick, scaly, brown skin. They looked like lizards crossed with humans. They had flat faces, but large mouths filled with sharp teeth. I had no idea what DNA had been spliced together to create them, but they were ugly and menacing. They were several inches taller than Jameson, and bulkier.

They'd stripped us of our armor and weapons. We were tied back to back, sitting on the ground.

"You okay?" Jameson asked.

"Fine. Having a great time."

His fingers brushed mine and squeezed.

I sighed. "I'm all right."

Night had fallen. The two monsters had a small fire going, and were cooking some sort of animal. Maybe a wallaby.

Every now and then, they grunted to each other.

"Jameson, are they...talking?"

"No fucking clue." His tone was not happy. "But it seems that way."

I'd always thought of the monsters as dangerous, slavering beasts that didn't really think. These two seemed to be communicating, cooking over a fire, working together, taking us prisoner.

Why? What was the plan? Did they even have one?

"I think it's worse than these two working together," Jameson said. "I think the aquatic monster brought us here."

"What?" I whispered. "Are you thinking it could communicate with these guys as well?"

"We did see evidence that the smaller one met with some other monsters."

A cold chill slithered through me. "If they're working together, to what end?"

"I don't know. I'm just speculating. Could be they're just planning a big cookout, and we're on the menu."

I stifled a slightly hysterical laugh. "I hope not."

"We aren't going to find out. We're going to get free."

I realized his hands were moving. "Can you untie the ropes?"

"I'm going to try. I'm getting you out of here."

I smiled at the fierceness in his voice. "*We're* getting out of here."

His fingers squeezed mine again. "Yeah. And Hunter Squad will find us. I know it."

There was rock-solid certainty in his voice. He trusted his squad that much.

"I have a tracker in my armor."

My pulse leaped. "It'll lead them straight to us."

"Not exactly. The satellite system isn't large enough yet, so the coverage is spotty. They'd need to be fairly close to us to pick up the signal."

My shoulders sagged. *Damn*.

"They'll be searching for us, Greer. I promise. They won't give up."

I relaxed against him. Jameson was with me. I wasn't alone. He'd always had such a strong, trustworthy feel, even when he'd been a teenager. Even then, he'd been taller and broader than everyone else.

"We sure as hell are getting out of here. I have several days of unbridled sex ahead of me. You promised."

His low laugh made me smile.

"And all those fantasies you said you've been collecting. I want to experience every one of them."

"I've been collecting them for years."

My heart knocked against my ribs. "Years?"

He was quiet for a moment. "I think the first one was when you were far too young. The moment I realized that Greer Baird had breasts."

I sucked in a breath. "You've wanted me that long?"

A beat of silence. "Yeah."

I stared blindly at the trees. "Why didn't you say anything?"

"So many reasons. You were younger than me. Then you were studying and working, and the next thing I knew, you had a boyfriend." He paused. "Albert or something."

"Alfie. I met him in one of my engineering classes." My gaze narrowed. "He came to a family barbecue once, then would never come again."

"I possibly gave him a talking to about respect and treating you right."

I laughed. "You must have scared the hell out of him. We broke up a few weeks later."

Jameson went quiet again. I was still trying to wrap my head around the fact that he'd liked me for so long.

"Mostly, I thought you wanted a smart guy, with degrees. I remember you and Alfie talking for ages about stuff that made my head spin."

"Jameson, you are one of the smartest men I know. Believe me, Alfie could not have held his own in our current situation. He couldn't have led his squad, saved me, and killed that monster. There are different kinds of smarts. Added to being brave, loyal, and a brilliant leader, I think that makes you pretty darn amazing, Jameson Steele."

"Shit, Greer." His voice was thick with emotion.

"And the muscles, don't forget those." I squeezed his fingers. "I *really* like your body."

Now he chuckled. "Happy to hear that. I'm pretty fond of yours too."

Just then, one of the monsters looked over at us. I stiffened. Its eyes glowing red in the darkness and it let out two guttural grunts.

The canine rose from where it was sleeping beside the fire. It loped over to us. It was far larger than a regular dog and had one red eye and one blue eye. Its shaggy fur was matted and when it snarled, I stared at its fangs.

My chest hitched. It could easily tear us apart. "Good doggie."

"Shh," Jameson warned.

It circled us and growled.

The monster by the fire grunted again, and the canine reluctantly returned to its master.

I let out a breath, and leaned back against Jameson.

"Try to get some sleep if you can," he said.

"I think that's impossible."

"We are getting out of here, Greer."

"That's right. I'm looking forward to those days off in your bed."

"Naked."

I went quiet for a moment. "Jameson, I'm going to fall in love with you."

He was silent for a moment. "Good. I'm already falling for you."

Warmth filled my chest. *God*. This man. This good, solid, strong man was mine. I felt it in my gut and my heart. I wanted to make him happy, hear him laugh, make a life together. He'd never hold me back, and he'd always support me.

Yes, I was going to fall in love with Jameson Steele.

But first, we had to escape and stay alive. I looked around at the thick darkness and even thicker bush. How the hell would Hunter Squad find us? Especially without tipping off our captors?

Jameson believed in them, and so would I.

"Get some rest, Greer. You'll need it. If we get free, we're going to need to move fast. And if my squad finds us first, we need to be ready."

I glanced at the monsters. "I'll try."

"I'll stay awake and keep watch. You're safe."

Such a good guy, and he was all mine. "Okay."

I was certain I would never fall asleep, but with the warmth of Jameson at my back, and knowing he was keeping watch, I found my eyelids drooping.

Shockingly, I drifted off to sleep.

CHAPTER FOURTEEN

Jameson

I felt the soft rise and fall of Greer's breaths.

I was glad she was getting some sleep. I watched the monsters. They were tearing into the meat and grunting.

They were definitely communicating. I felt more than a slight niggle of unease. They were working together, and I'd rarely seen that. Not in any coordinated way.

The Gizzida had been an intelligent, cunning species, but the hybrid monsters never had been. Growing up, I'd heard about the monster hunts. The squads had fought slavering beasts that only wanted to hunt and kill.

But I also knew the monsters had been breeding and mutating over the years.

Who knew what abilities those mutations had given them?

I tested the ropes on my wrists again. They were too tight and there was no give. A muscle in my jaw ticked. I really wanted to get Greer out of here.

Patience, Steele.

I sucked in a breath. The guys would come. I knew they'd be looking for us.

I had no idea what these monsters were planning to do with us. I didn't want to hang around to find out.

Greer made a small sound and settled again. The more sleep she had, the better. If we had to make a run for it, we'd need to move fast.

The monsters had thrown my weapons and armor into the water. They were smarter than they looked. The canine lifted its head and looked over my way.

In its one red eye, I saw hunger. It wanted to attack us.

Come closer and I'll take you down.

The creature sat back down, but one of the humanoid monsters rose. As it walked toward us, I tensed. I kept my gaze locked on it.

It came closer and made a grunting noise.

"You're going to die tonight," I said evenly. "I promise."

There was no sign it understood me. It leaned down and touched Greer's hair.

"Don't touch her," I snapped.

She jerked awake and made a gasping sound.

The monster stepped back, stared at me for a beat and bared its teeth. Skin flared around its neck, fluttering and menacing.

Shit. It reminded me of a frilled-neck lizard. They

used their neck frills to scare off predators. This monster must have some of the reptiles' DNA in it.

"*God*," Greer said.

The monster grunted, then it walked off into the trees.

If only I could get free, dammit. "It's okay, Greer."

"What did it want?" Her voice was uneven.

"It was just curious, I think." I heard her pulling in some deep breaths. "That's it. Just relax."

Silence fell again, and I saw the monster by the fire looked like it was napping.

Then I spotted movement in the darkness on the other side of the fire. I tensed. Was there another monster?

I let out a deep breath. Kai appeared, moving soundlessly on the other side of the fire. *Thank Christ*. Zeke also materialized out of the dark, moving in behind the monster still sitting by the flames. I couldn't see Marc or North, but I knew they'd be close.

"Greer," I whispered.

"Jameson?"

"Be ready."

"What—?" She looked toward the fire and gasped.

Zeke pulled a garrote over the monster's head. He yanked it back and the creature jerked, but Zeke pulled the wire harder.

The canine sprang up, but Kai was ready. He flung a knife at it, and the blade sliced into the dog's cheek. It let out a wild shriek, then sprinted for the trees.

Kai raced to help Zeke with the struggling monster. There were noises in the bushes right beside us.

My guess was, North and Marc were attacking the other humanoid that had gone into the trees.

Damn, I wanted to help, but the ropes weren't budging.

I tugged harder. "Come on."

Zeke and Kai had the monster pinned and Zeke was tugging hard on the garrote. I saw the creature's clawed feet hammering the ground, then it went still.

Kai leaped up and jogged over. "Hi."

"We've been waiting for you guys."

My friend pulled out a knife and cut us free. I took Kai's outstretched hand and let him pull me up. I ignored the multitude of aches and twinges in my body. We hugged and I slapped his back.

"We had no idea if you were alive," Kai said. "I'm damn glad to see you."

I helped Greer up.

Kai looked over at the remnants of the dead aquatic monster. "You did that?"

"Yeah, I was pissed. It almost drowned Greer."

"Greer, you all right?" Kai asked.

She nodded and hugged him.

Zeke appeared, coiling up his garrote wire. "You look no worse for wear, Jameson."

"I'm damn glad to see you guys."

Marc and North appeared, splattered in black blood. North was scowling and swiped at his hair. Marc was grinning.

"That didn't go quite to plan," Marc said.

"I'll say," North muttered.

Marc spread his arms. "The monster had frills on its neck. Wasn't expecting that. It is dead though."

"Marc, you're okay?" I asked, my gaze running over him.

"That tentacle had a tight grip on you," Greer said.

"Right as rain." He winked.

North made a scoffing sound. "He nearly died. He had broken ribs and internal injuries. I had to give him an emergency dose of nano-meds. He should be resting."

"Tattletale," Marc said.

"He insisted on coming," North added. "He's pumped full of painkillers and stimulants. When he crashes, he'll go down hard."

He'd come for me. I hadn't left him, and he wouldn't leave me. I met Marc's gaze and nodded. He nodded back. "How about we all get out of here?"

"I'll call in Colbie," Zeke murmured.

A howl filled the air.

We all swiveled and looked at the trees.

"I injured the canine monster, but it got away," Kai said. "It's hurt."

There was another howl. Then another answering one coming from a different direction. A second later, there was an entire chorus of howls.

Greer gasped, and my squad mates all stiffened.

"That's not good," Marc said.

"I need some weapons," I said. "The monsters tossed mine in the water. And someone give Greer a blaster."

Kai handed me a carbine. "Brought a spare for you."

I took it and checked it over as Marc gave Greer his

blaster. North handed me a combat knife. I strapped it to my thigh.

More howls echoed through the trees.

"We don't have time to wait for Colbie." I gripped the carbine. "We need to move. *Now*."

The men nodded.

"Form up and keep Greer in the middle." I touched her face. "You just need to focus on keeping up."

She swallowed. "I can do that."

I turned to face the trees. "Run."

Greer

I WAS RUNNING AS FAST as I could, Hunter Squad all around me. I swallowed. The night was filled with the haunting sounds of howls and excited yips.

The monster dogs were hunting us.

I focused on keeping up my speed. My lungs were already burning, as were the muscles in my legs. I didn't want to slow Jameson and the others down more than I already was. I knew they weren't running as fast as they could.

I sucked in air and focused on the forest ahead. It was so dark, and the only illumination came from small lights attached to the team's shoulders. Jameson had no armor on, but his face was etched with grim lines of determination.

Suddenly, carbine fire broke out behind me.

"Keep moving," Kai barked as he fired into the trees behind us.

God. The dogs sounded close.

There was a rush of something in the dark to the right. All of a sudden, a huge dog leaped through the air. Its red gaze was locked on me.

I stumbled and threw up my hands.

Jameson jumped in front of me.

The dog took him down, clawing at his chest. Before I could get my blaster up, Hunter Squad opened fire.

Oh, God. Jameson.

The dog's body jolted, and it slumped. Jameson pushed it off him.

"Fuck," he groaned.

Blood. There was so much blood.

"Jameson, no." I dropped down beside him. His chest was grooved with deep scratches and his ripped T-shirt was soaked with blood.

North knelt beside him, swinging a small backpack off his shoulders. He pulled out a small kit and tore it open.

Jameson's face was lined with pain. I stared blindly at all the blood, my heart beating fast and hard in my chest.

"I'm all right," he gritted out.

"You're clearly not." My voice was shrill.

"Someone give us some more light," North ordered.

Someone shifted and the beam of light illuminated just how bad the wounds were. I swallowed a cry.

"Here." North shoved some gauze at me. "Stop the worst of the bleeding. I'll give him an injection to slow the blood loss and increase healing."

I nodded, pressing down on the worst of Jameson's wounds. He grunted.

"I'm sorry," I whispered.

He reached up and cupped my cheek. "I'm tough. I promise."

North administered a pressure injection to the side of his neck.

I glanced at the dead dog. It was bigger than any old house pet. It was a weird, mutated thing—and possibly had some dingo in it—covered in orange fur mixed with shiny scales. It had a misshapen back, and its limbs didn't seem proportional.

More howls filled the night air.

"We've got to move," Kai said.

"I can run," Jameson said.

North cut Jameson's ruined shirt off, then pressed some suction bandages over the deep scratches. The others helped him to his feet.

He stood there, wavering a little, but I saw that fierce determination of his. "Let's move."

We started running again. I stayed close to his side. He wasn't moving with his usual athletic stride. His jaw was tight and he was gritting his teeth. I knew that he was in pain.

I pumped my arms and focused on running. The quicker we got out of here, the quicker he'd get proper medical treatment.

But the dogs were gaining on us. Their excited yips echoed through the forest.

"Incoming," Marc yelled.

"Form up," Jameson ordered, as he spun around.

The five men formed a shield in front of me. My heart lodged into my throat. Laser fire lit up the night.

Peeking between Jameson and Kai, I caught a glimpse of the pack. No two monster dogs were alike—some were giant, others smaller. They were all covered in a mix of scales and fur. They clearly had the DNA of various dog breeds.

"There are too many," Marc called out.

Jameson looked back at me. "Greer, run."

My chest locked. "Jameson—"

"Go. We'll give you a head start, and then we'll be right behind you."

I bit my lip. I knew if I stayed, I'd just distract him, but I didn't want to leave him. "You'd better be."

"Go, beautiful. Run as fast as you can."

My chest impossibly tight, I turned and ran.

Gripping my blaster, I did my best to see in the darkness. Air sawed in and out of my lungs. I tripped over some leaf debris and sticks, and nearly fell. I caught my balance and kept running. Branches slapped at my face and I shoved them out of my way.

I could hear the fighting in the distance but I kept running, worry choking me.

Please be all right.

There was a snap of a twig, followed by a low growl.

I stumbled to a stop, and it felt like barbed wire closed around my throat.

The growl came again.

I whirled.

A monster canine slunk out of the darkness. Its red gaze was locked on me.

My heart kicked my ribs and my fingers clenched on my blaster. It was at least as high as my waist, and its jaws were open, drool dripping off its fangs. It had a couple of patches of black fur, but most of it was covered in dark, scaly skin.

I lifted my weapon. I had no idea if it was enough to stop it.

"I'm not going to be your damn dinner."

The dog pounced.

I fired. I kept firing.

Blood splattered my face and chest, and the monster dropped at my feet.

The air rushed out of me. It was dead.

But before I could steady myself and keep going, there was more growling.

God, there were more of them coming. I glanced around and then ran to the nearest tree. I shoved the blaster in the waistband of my pants, then gripped the branches and pulled myself up. Twigs and leaves scratched at my arms, but I ignored them as I reached for a higher branch and hauled myself onto it.

Keep going, Greer. You stop and you're dead.

I climbed onto a thicker branch and sat on it. I glanced down and all the air left my lungs.

Three canine beasts were stalking around my tree, looking up at me.

Shit.

I swallowed and aimed my blaster at them.

I fired. They dodged the laser fire. One of them leaped and hit the tree. Its powerful body thudded against the trunk. The branch I was on shook.

Oh, God. With my free hand, I gripped the branch. I fired again, and the dog rammed the tree a second time.

The entire tree shook, and I slipped. The blaster fell from my fingers, and I cried out. My body tilted sideways and I reached out, trying to grab onto anything. I gripped the branch, but my legs slid over the edge, dangling below.

The canines leaped up, jaws snapping at my shoes. I yanked my legs up, but one dog clawed at my ankle. I cried out at the burning pain.

I felt my fingers start to slip.

No! I clutched at the rough bark. I didn't want to be torn apart by monster dogs.

Then, the sweet sound of carbine fire.

I looked down and saw laser fire hit the dogs. They yelped.

Jameson strode out of the trees, chest bare, his weapon aimed at the dogs. He looked like an avenging warrior angel.

Hunter Squad followed him.

Relief punched through me. *Thank God.*

CHAPTER FIFTEEN

HUNTER SQUAD

Jameson

I kept firing until the last canine threatening Greer was down.

I sprinted across the clearing, kicking the carcass of one monster dog out of my way. My body was filled with aches and pains, especially my chest, but the shot North had given me was holding back the worst of it. I knew I'd feel it later.

Greer was all that mattered. I needed to get to her.

"Greer."

"God, Jameson."

I held my arms up. "Let go and I'll catch you."

"I'll hurt your chest."

"You won't. I'll always catch you. Let go."

She did, and I caught her in my arms. Then I kissed her, pulling in the taste of her.

She was alive.

I'd been so afraid, knowing that she was in the bush

alone and that the dogs were hunting her. When I'd heard the blaster fire, my blood had run cold.

"Are they all dead?" she asked shakily.

"No." Even as I answered, distant barking echoed in the darkness. "Not all of them."

Her face blanched. "There are more?"

"The howls are bringing more out of hiding." Kai held out a blaster. "I think you dropped this."

Greer took it with a shaky smile.

"We need to stay ahead of them." I stroked her hair back. "Colbie is on her way."

Greer nodded. I put her down and she winced.

"Are you hurt?"

"It's just a scratch."

I saw blood on the torn bottom of her pants. "North."

The medic crouched. "It's not as bad as Jameson's scratches, but it's deep." He fished out an injector and pressed it to Greer's calf. "This will help."

"Can she run?" I asked.

"I'll run." She set her shoulders back. "I have no plans to be monster-dog dinner."

The growls and snarls of the dogs were closer now. Too damn close.

North finished wrapping a bandage around her ankle and rose. "That's all I can do for now."

Nodding, I took Greer's hand.

"Hunter Squad, let's get the hell out of here."

We ran. The trees blurred in the darkness as we sprinted. Greer was limping, but she didn't stop or slow down. The dogs got louder. *Fuck.* I heard them crashing through the bush.

We hit a clearing and I spotted an old building. It looked like some sort of maintenance structure. Maybe for the dam. It was dilapidated, and nearby were some mounds of sand and gravel that had weeds growing out of them.

We were halfway across the clearing when the pack of dogs broke the tree line.

My gut clenched. There were dozens of them.

So many. Too many.

Greer gasped. My squad turned and opened fire, all of us walking backward. I gripped my carbine as I sprayed the monsters with laser fire. Greer fired her blaster. I looked over and met Kai's gaze. I saw my own thoughts reflected in his eyes.

There were too many for us to fight.

We weren't going to make it.

Fuck that.

I never gave up. My parents had taught me that. I had too much to live for. My friends. My family. And this beautiful, strong woman fighting beside me.

I ripped my last grenade off my belt and tossed it.

Boom.

It exploded, several of the dogs yipped in pain.

But more kept coming.

Then a light speared across the clearing, blinding us.

"About damn time," Marc said.

The Talon swung into view overhead. The small auto-gun on the front of the quadcopter swiveled and laser fire traced across the monster dogs.

"Let's go!" I yelled.

The Talon lowered, the wash from the rotors flattening the grass as it hovered nearby. I yanked open the side door, leaped up, then held my hand out to Greer. I pulled her inside.

The others leaped aboard.

"Kai! Man the turret."

"I'm on it." He leaped into the main turret seat at the back. A second later, he opened fire on the monster dogs.

The Talon lifted into the night sky. We watched as Kai decimated the canines below.

"Take that, you ugly fuckers," Marc said.

Then, he staggered and collapsed into a seat.

"Marc," Zeke bit out.

Marc's head lolled. "Tired...so damn tired."

"I warned you, you idiot." North sat beside him as Marc slumped, unconscious. Our medic quickly checked his vitals. "He's fine. Pulse is strong." North fished around in his medical backpack, then pressed a monitoring patch to Marc's neck. "I'll keep an eye on him. He needs a second dose of nano-meds and bed rest."

I sat beside Greer, and she slumped against me.

"Well, Hunter Squad sure knows how to show a girl a good time."

I kissed the top of her head. She hadn't fallen apart. That strength of hers had held up. I reached out and rubbed some smeared blood off her face. Hell, it was probably my blood. "Want a job? We have a spot free."

She laughed. "Ah, no. I like my job just fine, thanks. Less monsters, gore, and fangs."

I hugged her tighter. "North, can you please check Greer's ankle again?"

She straightened. "No, check his chest first."

I shook my head. "I'm not getting checked until you've been checked."

She huffed out a breath. "You're as bad as my dad."

I grimaced. "I really hope you don't think of me and your dad in the same way."

She smiled, and even with her tangled hair, and dirt and blood smeared on her face, she looked beautiful. "Absolutely not."

North crouched in front of us. "You'll both need a shot of nano-meds when we get back." He wrapped a clean bandage around Greer's ankle, and I hated every wince she made. He turned to me. "You're next, Steele."

I leaned back and he pulled the bandages off my chest.

Greer hissed. I looked down and winced myself. It wasn't pretty. The claw gouges were ragged and uneven, the flesh was red and inflamed. My skin was streaked with blood.

North didn't blink an eye and set to work. He cleaned the wounds and they stung like hell. I tilted my head back and looked at the ceiling. Greer's fingers entwined with mine.

"I'll give you another shot of painkillers," North said.

I grunted. "Do it." My mind was whirring with everything I needed to do. "I need to organize the removal of the first monster carcass from the dam. And I want the area where I killed the second one scouted. There could be more of those lizard humanoids."

Greer squeezed my hand. "You need some rest, Jameson. Time to recover."

My gaze traced over her face. No, all I needed was

her. I smiled at her. "Kai, I'm leaving you in charge of that. I'm taking a few days off."

She beamed at me.

Kai leaned forward in the turret chair. "Don't worry, we'll take care of things. When was the last time you actually took time off?"

"Never. But I have a good reason to now."

Greer

HUMMING TO MYSELF, I finished putting snacks on the plate. Then I added some of the donuts I'd made yesterday. *Yum.* Luckily, we'd been burning off plenty of calories.

I grinned. I was standing in Jameson's kitchen, which looked like it didn't get much use. I was wearing one of his T-shirts. It swamped me, covering my naked body.

My scrapes, scratches, and bruises from the fight with the monsters had healed over the last three days. Now, I only had a few bruises from Jameson's fingers, scrapes from his stubble, and I was sensitive in certain places. I bit my lip. He'd lived up to the promise of keeping me naked in his bed. We'd spent most of the last three days there, and I'd loved every second of it.

And I was falling in love with him.

It was *amazing*.

"What's taking you so long?" He appeared in the doorway, shirtless, wearing only a soft pair of dark-blue, sleep pants.

Hello, muscles. I drank him in—his heavy chest, strong arms, muscled abs. I'd spent a lot of time stroking and kissing that body. Thankfully the nano-meds had healed him up and there were only a few pink lines left to show that he'd been injured. I knew that even those marks would be gone soon.

We'd survived.

"I'm adding a few donuts to the plate," I told him.

"Mmm, I love your donuts." He circled the island, and his arms wrapped around me from behind. He kissed the side of my neck, and I leaned into him.

"Almost as much as I love you," he murmured.

I spun and kissed him. "I'm falling hard and fast for you too, Jameson Steele. A part of me is kind of glad that aquatic monster turned up." I felt some sadness mixed with guilt. "But I still miss Sam and Travis. It doesn't seem right to be this happy when they're gone."

He cupped my cheeks. "Life goes on, baby. Our parents taught us that. It hasn't been easy since the alien invasion, but we're making strides. One day, all of the monsters will be gone, and we'll be safe. I'm dedicated to making that happen. I'm looking forward to the future." He grinned. "I'm looking forward to the day you give up your job and have lots of my babies."

I slapped his chest. "Very funny."

He gave a low chuckle and lifted me up on the counter. "I want you, Greer. In my life. One day, we'll get married and have babies. I think we should just start with one, and see how it goes with our work."

"I'd like that," I murmured. I wanted sturdy boys

with hazel-green eyes, and little girls with their daddy's smile.

"From here on out, it's you and me." He rubbed his nose against mine. "Us. We're going to make a life together. I'll make you happy, and I'll love you every way I know how."

"I'll be your friend, partner, and lover, Jameson. Yours. At your side, no matter what. I'll love you the way you deserve."

His mouth took mine, and within seconds, the kiss deepened.

"Right now, I think we need to go back to bed," he murmured against my lips.

"What about the food?" I gasped. His lips trailed down my neck and I dropped my head back.

He snatched up a donut and ate it in two bites. "We'll get it later." One big hand snaked under my shirt, sliding up my thigh. "I have tastier things to eat right now."

Just then, a chime rang through the house.

Jameson muttered a curse.

"Is that the front door?"

"Whoever it is will go away," he growled.

I heard a beep as the front door opened.

"I hope you're all decent," Sasha's voice chimed.

"Because we're coming in," Kai said.

I scrambled off the counter, tugged the hem of the shirt down, then finger-combed my hair. Jameson muttered another curse, just before the kitchen filled with people.

Hunter Squad, along with Sasha and Colbie bustled in.

Sasha set some plates on the counter, and Kai went straight to the fridge with a bag.

"We've got everything we need for a barbecue." Kai grinned at us, his teeth white against his brown skin.

"I don't want a barbecue," Jameson complained.

"Too bad," Sasha said. "You two have been holed up in here long enough." She grabbed some glasses from Jameson's cupboards, then whipped a bottle of white wine from her bag. "Greer, would you like a glass?"

"Sure."

Jameson wrapped an arm around my middle. "Don't encourage them."

"Greer, you are glowing." Marc grinned at me. "Something must agree with you. Can't be our grumpy leader."

Jameson growled.

"Don't mind Marc." Colbie perched on a stool. "He's only been awake for the last three hours. He's been unconscious the rest of the time." She shot him a narrow look.

"Just getting my beauty sleep, sparrow."

She sniffed. "It didn't work."

"But you're all healed?" Jameson asked.

Marc nodded. "One hundred percent, boss man. Nothing can slow me down, especially not a giant tentacle monster."

Behind him, North gave Jameson a small nod.

"We've got meat that needs to go on the grill," Kai said. "And I begged my sister for some salad greens from the gardens. She took pity on me and made us a fresh salad."

"I brought bread rolls and a pasta salad," Colbie added.

"I'll go and start the grill." Zeke headed for the back door to the patio.

"I'll open the beer," Marc said.

Jameson sighed. "You guys aren't going to leave, are you?"

I knew he wasn't really annoyed. His squad mates were his friends, his family.

"Nope," Marc answered cheerfully. "Besides, you and Greer have had more than enough sex for now. You need to eat."

I stifled a laugh.

"Fine." Jameson gripped my waist, then lifted me.

I let out a cry as he tossed me over his broad shoulder. "Jameson!"

"We're going to get dressed. Don't wreck my house while we're gone."

I heard everyone laughing as he carried me down the hallway. His hand slid under the shirt and caressed my butt as we headed back to the bedroom.

Laughing, I felt light and love fill me.

CHAPTER SIXTEEN

Jameson

I groaned, my hands clamped on Greer's hips as she rode me. "God, you're beautiful."

She pressed her hands to my chest, rocking with my cock lodged deep inside her. "I think you're beautiful." Her voice was husky. "In a rugged, tough way." She leaned down, her hair like a curtain around us. "And you're mine. Your hard body, your cock, and your heart and soul."

"All yours." I groaned again. "*Always.*"

She moved faster. I lifted my hips up and felt her pussy tightening. I reached out, my hand running over her flat belly, then delving between her thighs. I thumbed her clit.

"*Jameson.*" She screamed my name and tossed her head back.

Pure beauty. With a growl, I gripped her hips and

yanked her down. Deep inside her warmth, I poured myself inside her.

Wrung out, and floating on the wave of pleasure, I watched as she collapsed on top of me. My chest was rising and falling, and her warm breath puffed against my pec. She kissed my almost-healed wounds, and I ran a hand down her back.

Life was pretty damn perfect.

The echo of a knock thumped against my front door. I frowned. The knock turned to a hard hammering.

I sat up. "That better not be the guys again."

We'd had fun with the impromptu barbecue yesterday, but I hadn't had my fill of Greer yet. I wanted her all to myself.

"If it was the guys, they would have let themselves in," she said.

True. The knocking continued.

Who could that be?

"Someone wants to see you badly." She squinted at me. "It had better not be a woman, Jameson Steele."

"There's only one woman for me." I leaned over and kissed her.

The knocking stopped, then started again.

Muttering, I climbed out of bed. Greer followed and grabbed my T-shirt. I was distracted by her sweet ass as I pulled my pants on. I grabbed my communicator off the beside table to check the front door security feed. "Maybe if we ignore them, they'll go away." An image filled the screen, and I stiffened. "Or not."

"Who is it?"

I rubbed the back of my neck. "Um, my dad."

"Oh?" She finger-combed her hair. It was a messy blonde cloud around her makeup-free face.

"And your dad."

Her blue eyes widened. "Uh-oh."

"You finish up, I'll talk to them."

"No. Jameson, wait for me—"

I hurried out of the bedroom. I strode through the house, trying to think about what I'd say to the father of the woman I'd just spent the best part of three days fucking.

I paused at the front door. *Nope, I had nothing.* I sucked in a breath.

I touched a palm to the lock and the door opened. "Dad. Uncle Shaw."

Dad was an older, harder version of me. He was solidly built, and I knew he'd happily still lead a squad, if Mom hadn't asked him to take fewer risks and slow down. There was a scar on his face that a Gizzida raptor had given him in the early days of the invasion. He was scowling. Uncle Shaw was scowling too.

"Jameson." Shaw crossed his arms. "Where is my daughter?"

"Greer? Well..."

She breezed out of the hallway. "I'm here."

She'd brushed her hair, but she was still only wearing my T-shirt.

Hell.

Uncle Shaw's gaze narrowed and swung to me. "You're sleeping with my daughter?"

Dad frowned. "Jameson."

Greer came to my side and slid an arm around me. I rested mine over her shoulders.

"Honestly, we haven't been doing much sleeping," Greer said.

I winced.

Shaw's face darkened.

I held up a hand. "I'm falling in love with her."

Silence fell.

She smiled up at me. "And I feel the same."

"Hell," my father said. "I need a drink."

"It's nine o'clock in the morning, Dad," I said.

"So?" he replied.

"Fine." Shaw shouldered past us. "I need one, too."

Dad followed him.

Greer's eyes twinkled.

"We haven't been doing much sleeping? Really? Do you want your father to kill me?"

Her smile widened. "He loves you. He isn't going to kill you." She tugged me toward the kitchen.

"You clearly are not a man or a father," I muttered.

The dads had found my bourbon and glasses, and were pouring themselves generous amounts at the kitchen island. It was the good stuff, too. Pre-invasion. It had cost me a small fortune.

Shaw knocked back the glass. "Damn, that is good." He lowered his glass and pinned me with a glare.

I straightened. "I know I'm not good enough for her—"

"You're not," he said.

My dad growled. "Baird."

Greer crossed her arms. "He is. He saved me, he fought for me. He leaped out of a Talon and into the water with a giant monster to save me. He gave me CPR, and fought countless other dangerous creatures to keep me safe." She gripped my arm. "There is no braver, more courageous man than this one. Add to that, he's kind and thoughtful." She looked up at me. "And he's mine."

"Beautiful..." I cupped her cheek.

"Hell, they are in love," Shaw grumbled.

"Yep." Dad sipped his drink again.

"Jameson." Shaw waited until I looked at him. "I was going to say that no one is good enough for my little girl." He tugged her toward him. "But if I had to pick someone, you'd be it. I've watched you grow up, watched you turn into a good man and an excellent squad leader. I'm happy for both of you."

Relief flooded me.

"*Dad.*" She hugged him.

My dad gripped my shoulder. "You picked a hell of a woman."

"I didn't pick, it just...hit me. I knew that Greer was mine."

"I know the feeling." A small smile played on Dad's lips.

Greer came back to me.

"Hell," Dad said. "When they have kids, we'll be...grandfathers."

Shaw got a funny look on his face. "Shit." He poured himself another drink. Then he shook his head and pinned me with a look. "If you hurt her..."

"Stop it, Dad," Greer said.

"What's going on here?" a smoky female voice said.

Greer spun. "*Mom*. Please tell Dad to stop threatening Jameson."

Claudia Baird stood in the doorway, her hands on her hips. She was tall and fit, and the only sign of her age were the elegant gray strands threaded through her black hair that was up in a tight ponytail. Her face was set in tough lines. I was well aware that she could probably kick my ass.

"Jameson and I are together." Greer smiled. "I'm falling in love with him."

My chest swelled. Hell, I loved being claimed by her.

"Baird, stop threatening your future son-in-law," Claudia said.

Greer pulled a face at her father.

Then Claudia caught my gaze. "If you hurt my baby, you won't need to worry about Shaw, because I will hurt you. Badly and painfully."

I swallowed.

"Mom!" Greer said.

My dad lifted his glass. "Let's pour some more drinks."

Claudia's badass face morphed into a smile. "Pour me one too, Marcus. Looks like we're celebrating."

Then Greer pressed her face to my chest, holding me tight. She was smiling.

North

JAMESON

"I'M happy for the two of you, Jameson."

"Thanks, North."

These days, it seemed that Jameson had a permanent grin on his face. As we headed into the squad room at Squad Command, I shook my head.

Greer and Jameson had wasted no time since they'd fallen in love. She'd moved into his place, and was back at work on the dam project. But I knew she was coming back home to stay with him every few days.

I was glad my friends were in love.

It wasn't something I wanted, but I was happy for them. I didn't want anything that took me away from my work. I'd dedicated myself to being a doctor and a soldier.

I didn't have room for anything else.

When you took your eye off the ball, things got dropped, and people died.

"What was the reaction to your report on the monsters communicating and appearing to work together?" I asked. I knew Jameson had been in several meetings with the squad generals to discuss the latest monster behaviors.

Jameson's smile dissolved. "The brass aren't happy. Apparently, they're starting to get reports about this kind of thing happening in other places, too."

"Jesus." This couldn't be good. If the monsters started coordinating their attacks, they'd be exponentially more dangerous. "So, who's this new recruit we're meeting today?"

"Some distant relative of Cruz's. He recommended her to join the squad."

"Her?"

"Yep. She's his niece or second cousin, or second cousin's niece. Apparently, she's a good soldier, and also some sort of monster expert. She ran some studies on them over in the United States."

I frowned. "Do we really want someone on our squad who's not from here? She doesn't know the area, or our monsters."

Jameson shrugged. "If she can handle a carbine, I'm okay with it."

We rounded the corner, and I spotted Cruz Ramos. Cruz had been the second-in-command of Hell Squad, and was Jameson's dad's best friend. My sister said he had a handsome silver-fox vibe going on, especially when he played guitar at Hemi's.

Kai, Marc, and Zeke were with him. Marc was laughing with a woman whose back was to me. She was wearing brown cargo pants and a black T-shirt. She was tiny, but curvy. Her black hair was in a ponytail.

As I approached, she turned. Huge, dark eyes met mine.

I felt like I'd been hit by a grenade.

She had strong features, and freckles across her nose and cheeks. Her lips were plump and full.

"Ah, here are Jameson and North," Cruz said. "Jameson is the head of Hunter Squad, and North is the squad medic. Gentlemen, this is my niece."

"Sort of niece," the woman said with a wide smile.

Cruz waved a hand. "Family is family. Boys, this is Jessica Ramos."

"It's just Jess." She held a hand out to Jameson. "It's a

pleasure to meet you. I've heard so much about Hunter Squad. You and your team have quite the reputation."

I watched as they shook hands. Then, she turned to me. As soon as our hands touched, I felt a zap of electricity.

Shit, what was that?

Her dark eyes narrowed, and she pulled her hand back.

"Pleasure," I said.

"You flew over from San Diego?" Jameson asked. "You've been based there, right?"

She nodded. "Yes. San Diego is the base for the west coast monster hunting squads. I did work from Canada down to Mexico."

"How was the flight over?" Marc said.

"Fine. I was on a military flight with refueling in Hawaii. We had to make a slight detour for some monster activity in the central Pacific, but all in all, the flight wasn't too bad. I'm really glad to be here." She turned to her uncle. "And to meet all of the legendary Hell Squad."

Cruz winked. "Santha and I are so glad you're here. Jess has also been studying the monsters, learning about all of the hybrids, and finding new ways to eliminate them."

She nodded. "I have degrees in zoology and anthropology. I did my research thesis on the monsters in the Monterey area of California. On their habitat, hunting, and breeding behaviors."

"I think Jess should be able to give us some insight on these new behaviors you've been seeing," Cruz said.

"I don't think these changes make a difference." I met her gaze. "Shoot them and kill them."

"That's what we've been doing for thirty years," she said. "But I think they're evolving. We need to understand them, if we're ever going to completely eradicate them."

"Jess, I need to warn you that our final spot on the squad…" Jameson grimaced. "We haven't been able to keep any recruits for long."

Marc grinned. "Some might say it's cursed."

She smiled at him. "I'm always up for a challenge."

I frowned. I wasn't sure how I felt about her being on the squad. We had a rhythm that worked for us. We'd all grown up together and knew each other well. A stranger might upset the balance.

It could get people killed.

My gut tightened. That was something I wouldn't let happen. Not on my watch.

Jameson nodded. "Then welcome to Hunter Squad."

A siren sounded, blaring through the base.

"And it looks like you're going to get a trial by fire. That's our callout." Jameson turned. "Hunter Squad, suit up."

Jess met my gaze, and her smile held a hint of challenge. The others walked away, leaving just the two of us.

"I hope you're as good as they say," I said.

Her chin lifted. "I am."

"This squad, those men…they're like brothers to me."

"It doesn't matter who's on my squad, I'll always have their back."

I stared into her dark eyes for a beat. "I guess I'll need to see it to believe it."

She gave me one last look, then strode ahead of me, walking confidently, her ponytail swaying.

I shook my head. My gut said that Jessica Ramos would last about as long as our last few recruits.

Before I knew it, she'd be gone.

Blowing out a breath, I fought back my reaction to her. I needed to get my mind off our latest recruit, and onto the monster we had to kill.

I hope you enjoyed Greer and Jameson's story!

Hunter Squad continues with **NORTH**, coming in April 2025. Stay tuned for more monster-hunting action.

If you'd like to know more about the alien invasion, Marcus Steele, and Hell Squad, then check out the first Hell Squad book, *Marcus*. **Read on for a preview of the first chapter.**

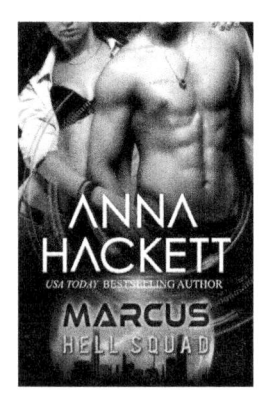

Don't miss out! For updates about new releases, free books, and other fun stuff, sign up for my VIP mailing list and get your *free box set* containing three action-packed romances.

Visit here to get started: www.annahackett.com

Would you like a FREE BOX SET of my books?

PREVIEW: MARCUS

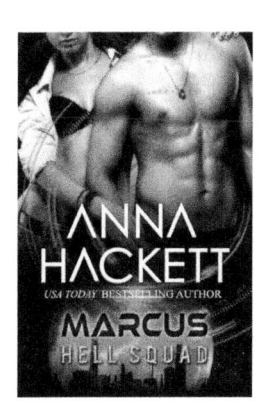

Her team was under attack.

Elle Milton pressed her fingers to her small earpiece. "Squad Six, you have seven more raptors inbound from the east." Her other hand gripped the edge of her comp screen, showing the enhanced drone feed.

She watched, her belly tight, as seven glowing red dots converged on the blue ones huddled together in the burned-out ruin of an office building in downtown

Sydney. Each blue dot was a squad member and one of them was their leader.

"Marcus? Do you copy?" Elle fought to keep her voice calm. No way she'd let them hear her alarm.

"Roger that, Elle." Marcus' gravelly voice filled her ear. Along with the roar of laser fire. "We see them."

She sagged back in her chair. This was the worst part. Just sitting there knowing that Marcus and the others were fighting for their lives. In the six months she'd been comms officer for the squad, she'd worked hard to learn the ropes. But there were days she wished she was out there, aiming a gun and taking out as many alien raptors as she could.

You're not a soldier, Ellianna. No, she was a useless party-girl-turned-survivor. She watched as a red dot disappeared off the screen, then another, and another. She finally drew a breath. Marcus and his team were the experienced soldiers. She'd just be a big fat liability in the field.

But she was a damn good comms officer.

Just then, a new cluster of red dots appeared near the team. She tapped the screen, took a measurement. "Marcus! More raptors are en route. They're about one kilometer away. North." God, would these invading aliens ever leave them alone?

"Shit," Marcus bit out. Then he went silent.

She didn't know if he was thinking or fighting. She pictured his rugged, scarred face creased in thought as he formulated a plan.

Then his deep, rasping voice was back. "Elle, we need an escape route and an evac now. Shaw's been hit in the leg, Cruz is carrying him. We can't engage more raptors."

She tapped the screen rapidly, pulling up drone images and archived maps. *Escape route, escape route.* Her mind clicked through the options. She knew Shaw was taller and heavier than Cruz, but the armor they wore had slim-line exoskeletons built into them allowing the soldiers to lift heavier loads and run faster and longer than normal. She tapped the screen again. *Come on.* She needed somewhere safe for a Hawk quadcopter to set down and pick them up.

"Elle? We need it now!"

Just then her comp beeped. She looked at the image and saw a hazy patch of red appear in the broken shell of a nearby building. The heat sensor had detected something else down there. Something big.

Right next to the team.

She touched her ear. "Rex! Marcus, a rex has just woken up in the building beside you."

"Fuck! Get us out of here. Now."

Oh, God. Elle swallowed back bile. Images of rexes, with their huge, dinosaur-like bodies and mouths full of teeth, flashed in her head.

More laser fire ripped through her earpiece and she heard the wild roar of the awakening beast.

Block it out. She focused on the screen. Marcus needed her. The team needed her.

"Run past the rex." One hand curled into a tight fist, her nails cutting into her skin. "Go through its hiding place."

"Through its nest?" Marcus' voice was incredulous. "You know how territorial they are."

"It's the best way out. On the other side you'll find a railway tunnel. Head south along it about eight hundred meters, and you'll find an emergency exit ladder that you can take to the surface. I'll have a Hawk pick you up there."

A harsh expulsion of breath. "Okay, Elle. You've gotten us out of too many tight spots for me to doubt you now."

His words had heat creeping into her cheeks. His praise...it left her giddy. In her life BAI—before alien invasion—no one had valued her opinions. Her father, her mother, even her almost-fiancé, they'd all thought her nothing more than a pretty ornament. Hell, she *had* been a silly, pretty party girl.

And because she'd been inept, her parents were dead. Elle swallowed. A year had passed since that horrible night during the first wave of the alien attack, when their giant ships had appeared in the skies. Her parents had died that night, along with most of the world.

"Hell Squad, ready to go to hell?" Marcus called out.

"Hell, yeah!" the team responded. "The devil needs an ass-kicking!"

"Woo-hoo!" Another voice blasted through her headset, pulling her from the past. "Ellie, baby, this dirty alien's nest stinks like Cruz's socks. You should be here."

A smile tugged at Elle's lips. Shaw Baird always knew how to ease the tension of a life-or-death situation.

"Oh, yeah, Hell Squad gets the best missions," Shaw added.

Elle watched the screen, her smile slipping. Everyone called Squad Six the Hell Squad. She was never quite sure if it was because they were hellions, or because they got sent into hell to do the toughest, dirtiest missions.

There was no doubt they were a bunch of rebels. Marcus had a rep for not following orders. Just the previous week, he'd led the squad in to destroy a raptor outpost but had detoured to rescue survivors huddled in an abandoned hospital that was under attack. At the debrief, the general's yelling had echoed through the entire base. Marcus, as always, had been silent.

"Shut up, Shaw, you moron." The deep female voice carried an edge.

Elle had decided there were two words that best described the only female soldier on Hell Squad—loner and tough. Claudia Frost was everything Elle wasn't. Elle cleared her throat. "Just get yourselves back to base."

As she listened to the team fight their way through the rex nest, she tapped in the command for one of the Hawk quadcopters to pick them up.

The line crackled. "Okay, Elle, we're through. Heading to the evac point."

Marcus' deep voice flowed over her and the tense muscles in her shoulders relaxed a fraction. They'd be back soon. They were okay. He was okay.

She pressed a finger to the blue dot leading the team. "The bird's en route, Marcus."

"Thanks. See you soon."

She watched on the screen as the large, black shadow of the Hawk hovered above the ground and the team boarded. The rex was headed in their direction, but they were already in the air.

Elle stood and ran her hands down her trousers. She shot a wry smile at the camouflage fabric. It felt like a dream to think that she'd ever owned a very expensive, designer wardrobe. And heels—God, how long had it been since she'd worn heels? These days, fatigues were all that hung in her closet. Well-worn ones, at that.

As she headed through the tunnels of the underground base toward the landing pads, she forced herself not to run. She'd see him—them—soon enough. She rounded a corner and almost collided with someone.

"General. Sorry, I wasn't watching where I was going."

"No problem, Elle." General Adam Holmes had a military-straight bearing he'd developed in the United Coalition Army and a head of dark hair with a brush of distinguished gray at his temples. He was classically handsome, and his eyes were a piercing blue. He was the top man in this last little outpost of humanity. "Squad Six on their way back?"

"Yes, sir." They fell into step.

"And they secured the map?"

God, Elle had almost forgotten about the map. "Ah, yes. They got images of it just before they came under attack by raptors."

"Well, let's go welcome them home. That map might just be the key to the fate of mankind."

They stepped into the landing areas. Staff in various military uniforms and civilian clothes raced around. After the raptors had attacked, bringing all manner of vicious creatures with them to take over the Earth, what was left of mankind had banded together.

Whoever had survived now lived here in an underground base in the Blue Mountains, just west of Sydney, or in the other, similar outposts scattered across the planet. All arms of the United Coalition's military had been decimated. In the early days, many of the surviving soldiers had fought amongst themselves, trying to work out who outranked whom. But it didn't take long before General Holmes had unified everyone against the aliens. Most squads were a mix of ranks and experience, but the teams eventually worked themselves out. Most didn't even bother with titles and rank anymore.

Sirens blared, followed by the clang of metal. Huge doors overhead retracted into the roof.

A Hawk filled the opening, with its sleek gray body and four spinning rotors. It was near-silent, running on a small thermonuclear engine. It turned slowly as it descended to the landing pad.

Her team was home.

She threaded her hands together, her heart beating a little faster.

Marcus was home.

Marcus Steele wanted a shower and a beer.

Hot, sweaty and covered in raptor blood, he leaped down from the Hawk and waved at his team to follow. He kept a sharp eye on the medical team who raced out to tend to Shaw. Dr. Emerson Green was leading them, her white lab coat snapping around her curvy body. The blonde doctor caught his gaze and tossed him a salute.

Shaw was cursing and waving them off, but one look from Marcus and the lanky Australian sniper shut his mouth.

Marcus swung his laser carbine over his shoulder and scraped a hand down his face. Man, he'd kill for a hot shower. Of course, he'd have to settle for a cold one since they only allowed hot water for two hours in the morning in order to conserve energy. But maybe after that beer he'd feel human again.

"Well done, Squad Six." Holmes stepped forward. "Steele, I hear you got images of the map."

Holmes might piss Marcus off sometimes, but at least the guy always got straight to the point. He was a general to the bone and always looked spit and polish. Everything about him screamed money and a fancy education, so not surprisingly, he tended to rub the troops the wrong way.

Marcus pulled the small, clear comp chip from his pocket. "We got it."

Then he spotted her.

Shit. It was always a small kick in his chest. His gaze traveled up Elle Milton's slim figure, coming to rest on a face he could stare at all day. She wasn't very tall, but that didn't matter. Something about her high cheekbones, pale-blue eyes, full lips, and rain of chocolate-brown hair...it all worked for him. Perfectly. She was beautiful, kind, and far too good to be stuck in this crappy underground maze of tunnels, dressed in hand-me-down fatigues.

She raised a slim hand. Marcus shot her a small nod.

"Hey, Ellie-girl. Gonna give me a kiss?"

Shaw passed on an iono-stretcher hovering off the ground and Marcus gritted his teeth. The tall, blond sniper with his lazy charm and Aussie drawl was popular with the ladies. Shaw flashed his killer smile at Elle.

She smiled back, her blue eyes twinkling and Marcus' gut cramped.

Then she put one hand on her hip and gave the sniper a head-to-toe look. She shook her head. "I think you get enough kisses."

Marcus released the breath he didn't realize he was holding.

"See you later, Sarge." Zeke Jackson slapped Marcus on the back and strolled past. His usually-silent twin, Gabe, was beside him. The twins, both former Coalition Army Special Forces soldiers, were deadly in the field. Marcus was damned happy to have them on his squad.

"Howdy, Princess." Claudia shot Elle a smirk as she passed.

Elle rolled her eyes. "Claudia."

Cruz, Marcus' second-in-command and best friend from their days as Coalition Marines, stepped up beside Marcus and crossed his arms over his chest. He'd already pulled some of his lightweight body armor off, and the ink on his arms was on display.

The general nodded at Cruz before looking back at Marcus. "We need Shaw back up and running ASAP. If the raptor prisoner we interrogated is correct, that map shows one of the main raptor communications hubs." There was a blaze of excitement in the usually-stoic general's voice. "It links all their operations together."

Yeah, Marcus knew it was big. Destroy the hub, send the raptor operations into disarray.

The general continued. "As soon as the tech team can break the encryption on the chip and give us a location for the raptor comms hub—" his piercing gaze leveled on Marcus "—I want your team back out there to plant the bomb."

Marcus nodded. He knew if they destroyed the raptors' communications it gave humanity a fighting chance. A chance they desperately needed.

He traded a look with Cruz. Looked like they were going out to wade through raptor gore again sooner than anticipated.

Man, he really wanted that beer.

Then Marcus' gaze landed on Elle again. He didn't keep going out there for himself, or Holmes. He went so people like Elle and the other civilian survivors had a chance. A chance to do more than simply survive.

"Shaw's wound is minor. Doc Emerson should have him good as new in an hour or so." Since the advent of the nano-meds, simple wounds could be healed in hours, rather than days and weeks. They carried a dose of the microscopic medical machines on every mission, but only for dire emergencies. The nano-meds had to be administered and monitored by professionals or they were just as likely to kill you from the inside than heal you.

General Holmes nodded. "Good."

Elle cleared her throat. "There's no telling how long it will take to break the encryption. I've been working with the tech team and even if they break it, we may not be able to translate it all. We're getting better at learning the raptor language but there are still huge amounts of it we don't yet understand."

Marcus' jaw tightened. There was always something. He knew Noah Kim—their resident genius computer specialist—and his geeks were good, but if they couldn't read the damn raptor language…

Holmes turned. "Steele, let your team have some downtime and be ready the minute Noah has anything."

"Yes, sir." As the general left, Marcus turned to Cruz. "Go get yourself a beer, Ramos."

"Don't need to tell me more than once, *amigo*. I would kill for some of my dad's tamales to go with it." Something sad flashed across a face all the women in the base mooned over, then he grimaced and a bone-deep weariness colored his words. "Need to wash the raptor off me, first." He tossed Marcus a casual salute, Elle a smile, and strode out.

Marcus frowned after his friend and absently started loosening his body armor.

Elle moved up beside him. "I can take the comp chip to Noah."

"Sure." He handed it to her. When her fingers brushed his he felt the warmth all the way through him. Hell, he had it bad. Thankfully, he still had his armor on or she'd see his cock tenting his pants.

"I'll come find you as soon as we have something." She glanced up at him. Smiled. "Are you going to rec night tonight? I hear Cruz might even play guitar for us."

The Friday-night gathering was a chance for everyone to blow off a bit of steam and drink too much homebrewed beer. And Cruz had an unreal talent with a guitar, although lately Marcus hadn't seen the man play too much.

Marcus usually made an appearance at these parties, then left early to head back to his room to study raptor movements or plan the squad's next missions. "Yeah, I'll be there."

"Great." She smiled. "I'll see you there, then." She hurried out clutching the chip.

He stared at the tunnel where she'd exited for a long while after she disappeared, and finally ripped his chest armor off. Ah, on second thought, maybe going to the rec night wasn't a great idea. Watching her pretty face and captivating smile would drive him crazy. He cursed under his breath. He really needed that cold shower.

As he left the landing pads, he reminded himself he should be thinking of the mission. Destroy the hub and kill more aliens. Rinse and repeat. Death and killing, that was about all he knew.

He breathed in and caught a faint trace of Elle's floral scent. She was clean and fresh and good. She always worried about them, always had a smile, and she was damned good at providing their comms and intel.

She was why he fought through the muck every day. So she could live and the goodness in her would survive. She deserved more than blood and death and killing.

And she sure as hell deserved more than a battled-scarred, bloodstained soldier.

Hell Squad
Marcus
Cruz

Gabe
Reed
Roth
Noah
Shaw
Holmes
Niko
Finn
Devlin
Theron
Hemi
Ash
Levi
Manu
Griff
Dom
Survivors
Tane
Also Available as Audiobooks!

ALSO BY ANNA HACKETT

Fury Brothers

Fury

Keep

Burn

Take

Claim

Also Available as Audiobooks!

Unbroken Heroes

The Hero She Needs

The Hero She Wants

The Hero She Craves

The Hero She Deserves

The Hero She Loves

Also Available as Audiobooks!

Sentinel Security

Wolf

Hades

Striker

Steel

Excalibur

Hex

Stone

Also Available as Audiobooks!

Norcross Security

The Investigator

The Troubleshooter

The Specialist

The Bodyguard

The Hacker

The Powerbroker

The Detective

The Medic

The Protector

Mr. & Mrs. Norcross

Also Available as Audiobooks!

Billionaire Heists

Stealing from Mr. Rich

Blackmailing Mr. Bossman

Hacking Mr. CEO

Also Available as Audiobooks!

Team 52

Mission: Her Protection

Mission: Her Rescue

Mission: Her Security

Mission: Her Defense

Mission: Her Safety

Mission: Her Freedom

Mission: Her Shield

Mission: Her Justice

Also Available as Audiobooks!

Treasure Hunter Security

Undiscovered

Uncharted

Unexplored

Unfathomed

Untraveled

Unmapped

Unidentified

Undetected

Also Available as Audiobooks!

Oronis Knights

Knightmaster

Knighthunter

Galactic Kings

Overlord

Emperor

Captain of the Guard

Conqueror

Also Available as Audiobooks!

Eon Warriors

Edge of Eon

Touch of Eon

Heart of Eon

Kiss of Eon

Mark of Eon

Claim of Eon

Storm of Eon

Soul of Eon

King of Eon

Also Available as Audiobooks!

Galactic Gladiators: House of Rone

Sentinel

Defender

Centurion

Paladin

Guard

Weapons Master

Also Available as Audiobooks!

Galactic Gladiators

Gladiator

Warrior

Hero

Protector

Champion

Barbarian

Beast

Rogue

Guardian

Cyborg

Imperator

Hunter

Also Available as Audiobooks!

Hell Squad

Marcus

Cruz

Gabe

Reed

Roth

Noah

Shaw

Holmes

Niko

Finn

Devlin

Theron

Hemi

Ash

Levi

Manu

Griff

Dom

Survivors

Tane

Also Available as Audiobooks!

The Anomaly Series

Time Thief

Mind Raider

Soul Stealer

Salvation

Anomaly Series Box Set

The Phoenix Adventures

Among Galactic Ruins

At Star's End

In the Devil's Nebula

On a Rogue Planet

Beneath a Trojan Moon

Beyond Galaxy's Edge

On a Cyborg Planet

Return to Dark Earth

On a Barbarian World

Lost in Barbarian Space

Through Uncharted Space

Crashed on an Ice World

Perma Series

Winter Fusion

A Galactic Holiday

Warriors of the Wind

Tempest

Storm & Seduction

Fury & Darkness

Standalone Titles

Savage Dragon

Hunter's Surrender

One Night with the Wolf

For more information visit www.annahackett.com

ABOUT THE AUTHOR

I'm a USA Today bestselling romance author who's passionate about ***fast-paced, emotion-filled*** contemporary romantic suspense and science fiction romance. I love writing about people overcoming unbeatable odds and achieving seemingly impossible goals. I like to believe it's possible for all of us to do the same.

I live in Australia with my own personal hero and two very busy, always-on-the-move sons.

For release dates, behind-the-scenes info, free books, and other fun stuff, sign up for the latest news here:

Website: www.annahackett.com

Printed in Great Britain
by Amazon